Clara a

For my better half.

Dear Santa,
All I want for Christmas is a fat wallet
and a skinny waist.
Please don't get them mixed up again
like you did last year...

December 1st

Stupid mittens. How are you supposed to grasp anything when your hands have been made into makeshift crab claws? Fumbling around in my bag for some cash, I allow my nostrils to lead me towards the delicious smell of hot mince pies. Tearing off a mitten with my teeth like a hungry penguin, I exchange a handful of coins for a steaming pie and lick my lips as the vendor spoons on a huge dollop of brandy cream. Nothing quite says Christmas like a good old mince pie.

Trudging through the cold snow, I sink my teeth into the delicious golden pastry. The sun has only just set and I have already consumed a ridiculous number of calories. My Starbucks Gingerbread Latte alone must have contained my entire daily allowance. Just thinking of those yummy red cups makes my mouth water uncontrollably. It just isn't Christmas without a Starbucks special, is it? Wiping sticky crumbs off my chin, I narrowly avoid knocking over a freshly built snowman. Who the hell builds a snowman in the middle of a busy shopping centre? Ignoring the cries of annoyed children, I flash their parents an apologetic smile as they hurriedly try to replace the carrot nose. I think it is safe to say that my maternal instincts haven't kicked in *just* yet.

The twinkling fairy lights that hang overhead provide a dazzling rainbow in the dark sky for the hordes of people that are buzzing along the busy street. It's almost like a festive firework display, signalling to the world that the Christmas period has arrived. I look up and smile at the giant flashing baubles that are draped in the bare trees which line the pavement. It would appear that the festive season is well and truly upon us. Frosty snowflakes land on my nose as I devour the last of my yummy treat. I *love* Christmas. The glistening decorations, the indulgent food and the one too many glasses of vino. I just love everything about it. I always have. Ever since I was a child and would peek down the stairs to see if Rudolf had been for his milk and cookies. I still get that buzz of excitement going to bed on Christmas Eve, even though I know the only fat man with rosy cheeks I will be seeing is my sleazy uncle.

Weaving between the crowds of avid shoppers, I clutch my handbag tightly to my chest. We haven't even put our tree up yet and already people are fighting over the latest gizmos and gadgets. I wonder what *must have* gifts are causing people to go crazy this year. I remember when my dad camped outside Argos on a cold December night because I just *had* to have a Tamagotchi. Stopping to peer into a frosty shop window, I rack my brains for the ideal gift to get my new husband for Christmas. Somehow, I don't think he would appreciate a handheld digital pet.

As this is our first Christmas together as man and wife I want to get him something extra special, but what exactly do you buy for the man who has everything? Yet more golf clubs? A watch to add to his ever-expanding collection? Perhaps another pair of cuff links to toss in the drawer along with the hundreds of others? Men are difficult to buy for at the best of times, but when you are married to a rich fashion designer it makes the task of shopping that little bit more demanding. Not that I am complaining, being married to a gorgeous American designer *is* kind of fabulous, even if I do say so myself.

Dragging myself away from the window, I tug my heavy handbag up onto my shoulder and carry on walking. My precious Hunter wellies make trekking in the terrible weather just about bearable. Slushy snow provides an icy blanket for the pavement, resulting in people doing a half walk, half twerk manoeuvre to stop them from losing their balance. Even though I opened the first window of my advent calendar this morning, I really can't believe that it's December already. It still feels like only yesterday that I was walking down the aisle. It's hard to imagine that it has been almost a year now. Just thinking back to my wedding day makes my stomach flutter uncontrollably. Sometimes I forget that I am really married. I, Clara Andrews, sorry, Clara *Morgan* am actually someone's wife. Before we said *I do*, I never thought that it would feel any different once I got that platinum band on my finger, but knowing that Oliver chose me over every other girl on the planet is the best feeling in the world. There really is something to be said about putting a ring on it.

Pulling my bobble hat over my cold ears, I push my way inside Debenhams and dig out my shopping list. Oliver's gift isn't the only thing that I've got to worry about this year as we have invited his parents to join us from Texas and now my own parents have decided to join us, too. And let's not forget Lianna, my best friend who is having an early mid-life crisis at the prospect of turning thirty single and homeless. With having a houseful to entertain, it's fair to say that I am a little apprehensive at being the hostess. Let's face it, the closest I've ever come to hosting the perfect dinner party is ordering a few take-out pizzas on a Friday evening and opening a bottle of red.

Telling myself that everything will be OK, I pick up a pair of feather mules and drop them into my basket. Now, you might think that a sexy pair of pink stilettos is a strange gift for my mother-in-law, but I know that Janie will absolutely *love* these. Making my way over to the homeware section, I turn back and toss in another pair of the fluffy slippers. On second thoughts, I should probably get some for my own mother, too. I really don't want handbags at dawn on Christmas morning. If you would have told me twelve months ago that I would be buying my mum gifts from the erotic lingerie section, I never would have believed you. Oh, how much can change in the space of one short year.

Stepping onto the escalator, I peer over the railing at the queue of overly excited children waiting to see Father Christmas. Proud parents click away with their cameras, desperate not to miss the obligatory *tell Santa what you would like for Christmas* shot. I let out a little snort as a tiny toddler stamps on an elf's foot and laughs hysterically when she shouts out in pain. It really is the most wonderful time of the year.

* * *

Pushing my way into the apartment, I drop my mountain of shopping bags onto the dining table and attempt to kick off my wellies. The ear-piercing screams that are drifting out of the living room can only mean one thing - The Strokers are here. Rubbing my hands together for warmth, I pad across the plush carpet and stretch my mouth into a smile. Oliver and Lianna aside, The Strokers are close contenders for my favourite people in the world. For those of you who don't know, Marc Stroker has been one of my closest friends for many years now. I still find it a little strange to see him with a wedding band on his finger and two babies in tow. However, I am the first person to admit that Gina, Madison and MJ are the best things that ever happened to him.

'Look at you!' Holding out my arms, I bend down and scoop up a jubilant Madison, who is happily tearing around the living room in a Cinderella costume.

She might only be a toddler, but Madison is already a mini Gina in the making. Her love for anything pink and sparkly has been apparent since day one and last week I'm sure that I heard her say *leopard print*. Madison's cheeks turn pink with glee as I throw her up in the air. One thing's for sure, Marc's black curls combined with Gina's big green eyes make for one very beautiful baby. Sticking my head into MJ's car seat, I stroke his red face gently. Unlike Madison, Marc Junior does *not* look happy.

'I think someone's hungry.' Gina coos, picking up the screaming baby and nuzzling his tiny nose.

'Awwh! He's getting *so* big.' Passing Madison over to Marc, I collapse into a heap on the couch. 'Where's Oliver?'

'He went to get pizza.' Marc replies, in-between blowing raspberries on Madison's stomach.

'Great! I'm starving. I haven't eaten a thing all day.' I lie, trying to erase the mince pie from my memory.

'How was the shopping?' He asks. 'I don't envy you braving the shops in this weather.'

'It was crazy. Everywhere was so cold and busy. I think I got the majority of things though. This year I am *determined* not to leave it to the last-minute like I normally do.' Trying not to look as Gina whips out a humongous boob and starts to feed a hungry MJ, I turn to face Marc. 'Have you made a start on your Christmas plans yet?'

'We're actually thinking of going to see Gina's parents this year. They haven't seen MJ yet and Gina's still on maternity leave...'

'Australia?' I raise my eyebrows impressed and try not to feel too envious. 'Wow!'

'Yeah.' He pushes his glasses up the bridge of his nose and looks down at the ground.

'I'm guessing that barbecues on the beach and kangaroos are going to be a little different to turkey and Brussels sprouts!' Laughing at the image of Marc wearing a cork hat whilst barbecuing shrimp, I reach for the television remote.

'Just a little.' Marc agrees. 'Aren't you having Lianna over this year?'

'We are.' I reply. 'She's been on a downer ever since Pablo left and between me and you, I don't think that she's taking her impending birthday all that well.' I roll my eyes as Marc nods in agreement.

'I honestly don't know what the big deal is. I was fine when I turned thirty.' He shrugs his shoulders and rocks Madison back and forth gently.

'Are you kidding me?' Gina chips in. 'When you turned thirty, you wouldn't get out of bed for a *week*!'

'I remember!' I laugh. 'You had a full-on meltdown! I'm just surprised that you didn't get a Porsche Boxster and a sleeve tattoo.'

'You just wait until you turn thirty, Andrews.'

'Actually, I think you will find it's *Morgan* now.' I flash him my wedding band and stick out my tongue.

'You will always be an Andrews in my eyes.' Marc passes me Madison as Oliver bursts into the apartment, his arms laden with takeout boxes.

'I got pizza!' Oliver hollers across the room. 'Who's hungry?'

Madison makes a squeal that resembles a happy piglet and rolls off my knee, making a beeline for the pizza. A chorus of cheers echo around the room as we all give in to the lure of greasy junk food. Tearing a sleepy MJ away from her chest, Gina slips him into a baby sling and takes a seat at the kitchen island. I watch proudly as Oliver dresses the table with plates, cutlery and glasses. He has slotted into the role of hubby perfectly.

'Hi.' I smile, accepting a plate of pizza. 'How are you?'

'Extremely cold!' He replies, shaking off his damp coat and pulling me in for a kiss. 'Successful shopping trip?'

Nodding in response, I take a seat at the table and smile as Marc carefully tears Madison's pizza up into bite sized pieces. Thankfully, MJ has drifted off into a milk induced sleep meaning that we can all enjoy our dinner in peace. Diving into my pizza, I take a huge bite and sit back in my seat, savouring the cheesy goodness. I still find it hard to believe how much we have all grown up. It's strange to think that Marc and Gina have two adorable children and Oliver and I have tied the knot. Kind of ironic when Li has always been the one of the group who knew *exactly* what she wanted out of life. No wonder she feels so down at the moment. It's such a shame that she is yet to find her happily ever after.

To say that Lianna has been dealt a bad hand in the love department would be an understatement. With her 30th birthday just two weeks away, Li has been rather hysterical about hitting the major milestone without a significant other to celebrate with. For the past couple of years, she had been on and off with the infamous Dan. This finally came to an end when the delightful Dan was caught in a rather compromising position with one of Oliver's cousins. Lianna was devastated by his betrayal and it took six months of fun in the sun with the gorgeous Pablo for her to get over Dan once and for all. Sadly for Li, Pablo decided to call it a day a few weeks ago and returned to his homeland of Tenerife. I would like to say that no one saw the demise of Pablo coming, but when do holiday romances ever really work out?

I cross my legs and think back to all the times that Li has been there for me over the years. The role of wife might be one that seems impossible to her, but she has always excelled in her role as best friend. Taking another bite of my pizza, I decide that 2016 is going to be Lianna's year and it all starts with a fantastic Christmas...

When someone asks,
'Where is your Christmas spirit?'
Is it wrong to point to the drinks
cabinet?

December 2nd

Waking up to the sound of torrential rain battering against the window is strangely soothing. The raindrops are loud and heavy as they thrash to the ground angrily. I peel open an eye and watch in fascination as a strong wind causes the trees outside to shake uncontrollably. Stretching out my legs, I roll over and snuggle into Oliver's warm back. I just *love* being tucked up in bed all toasty when the weather is frightful outside.

A quick glance at my watch reminds me that I am going to meet Lianna in little over an hour. If I had it my way I would stay here all day, but despite the terrible weather, Li has *got* to find somewhere to live. It was well over six months ago that she and Dan went their separate ways, but due to the unfortunate state of the economy, it has taken them until now to finally get a buyer for the house that they once shared. The real stinker of the situation is that the property sold for far less than they paid for it just a year earlier. Since then, Li has been sofa surfing at her parent's place and from what she has been telling me, she is starting to wear out her welcome. Shockingly, it turns out that Lianna has been getting over Pablo by getting *under* various different gentlemen. I can't say I am surprised that her poor mother has finally had enough.

Planting a kiss on Oliver's neck, I throw back the covers and begrudgingly roll out of bed. My feet feel like blocks of ice as I sleepily make my way towards the bathroom. I spend a few minutes washing and brushing before running back into the bedroom to frantically look around for some clothes. After dragging on a pair of skinny jeans and a fluffy jumper, I turn my attention to my face. I *really* need to apply some fake tan. The harsh December weather has not been kind to my skin at all. Trying to hide the dark circles with masses of Touché Éclat, I apply a quick sweep of blusher before reaching for my beloved UGG boots. When Gina first bought into the UGG craze, I swore blind that I wouldn't be seen dead in the clumpy eyesores. However, a drunken night at Lianna's which involved a broken stiletto and some serious hailstone was enough for me to borrow a pair. Since then I have acquired quite the collection and I'm not ashamed to say that they have taken pride of place in my wardrobe. Sorry, Dr Martens!

Not wanting to wake Oliver I scrawl out a quick note and stick it to the coffee maker, which is the only place in the entire apartment that I can be totally sure he won't miss it. With a quick spray of perfume, I toss the essentials into my handbag and make for the door. As I ride down to the ground floor, I pull on a pair of mittens and dig out my umbrella, bracing myself for the cold. Stepping out of the lift into the lobby, I am surprised to see Lianna's familiar blonde beehive heading for the stairs.

'Li!' I shout, waving my arms around to gain her attention.

Stopping midway up the staircase, Lianna spins around and frowns as she tries to pinpoint my voice.

'What are you doing here?' I raise my eyebrows at her choice of outfit as she makes her way over to me. 'I thought we were meeting at the first property?'

'We were, but Liam drives past this way on his way to work so I told him to drop me outside.' Trying not to fall in her ridiculously high wedges, she digs a compact mirror out of her handbag and wipes last night's mascara from under her eyes. I can't help noticing that she stinks of stale booze.

'Liam?' I crinkle my nose up in

confusion. 'Who the hell is Liam?'

'*Liam*.' Lianna retorts, as if it is totally obvious who Liam is. 'Liam from last weekend.'

'You mean the creepy guy from the kebab shop on Saturday night?' My horror is evident in the tone of my voice.

'He was *not* creepy!' She laughs loudly and pulls her coat tightly around her.

'You cannot be serious.' Shaking my head in disgust, I push her outside into the car park.

'Relax, Clara! I'm not going to marry the guy!' Li rolls her eyes and tops up her lip gloss, totally oblivious to how much this has perturbed me.

Lianna and I spent last Saturday evening in Lightning, a new cocktail bar in the city centre. One Margarita turned into ten and before we knew it, we were being accosted by a highly-intoxicated Welshman in a kebab shop. For some disturbing reason, Li decided to give him her number and even more worryingly, she actually agreed to meet up with him. Beeping open the car, I jump into the driver's seat and take my TomTom out of the glove compartment.

'All right, the first appointment is in... Greenton.' I confirm, looking at my print out of the properties we are going to view. 'Do you have the postcode?'

'1... S... Q... 8... P... L.' She couldn't sound more uncertain if she tried.

'Right... since when do postcodes start with numbers?' I roll my eyes and turn on the window wipers.

'Could you swing by McDonald's first?' Lianna yawns. 'I could murder a McMuffin.'

* * *

Looking at the putrid green walls dubiously, I glance over at Lianna for her reaction. When the estate agent said that this property was in need of a little facelift, I didn't realise what she really meant was that the whole place needed demolishing. Lianna shakes her head regrettably as the estate agent lets out an annoyed sigh. This must be the tenth property that she has shown us today and not one of them has even come close to being classed as liveable. From the damp apartment in the centre of town to the run down detached in the suburbs, it seems that Lianna's single person salary won't stretch half as far as she anticipated.

Before Lianna purchased her cool new-build with Dan, she lived in one of her parent's luxury apartments pretty much rent free. Marc and I were always so jealous that she got to live the life of luxury for a nominal donation each month. Unfortunately for Lianna, her property developer mother sold the apartment the second that Li moved out. Given that there's now a lovely Spanish family living in there, it seems there is no way back to her life of luxury. Thanking the estate agent for her time, we pull our hoods up over our heads and run to the car. Once safely inside and shielded from the heavy rain, I turn to face Lianna and try to be optimistic.

'The third one wasn't all that bad.'

'Are you kidding me?' Lianna laughs. 'The apartment opposite the soup kitchen with the leaky roof?'

'Come on, you're making it sound worse than it was.' Sighing loudly, I put the car into gear and pull out onto the road. 'I just think that we might have to reassess your requirements.'

'What do you mean?' She retorts angrily.

'I mean... I think that we might have to be a little more *realistic* as to what your budget can stretch to.'

'OK...' She replies slowly, with a face that says she couldn't disagree more.

'For instance, you don't *have* to have a private parking space and an en suite isn't exactly a necessity, is it?' Turning to face the window, Li folds her arms like a stroppy teenager. 'I understand that it's going to take a little bit of getting used to considering your previous accommodation, but we should be looking at this like a new beginning for you.'

'The beginning of the end more like.' Li scoffs.

'I disagree.' Stretching my face into a grin, I reach over and squeeze her knee encouragingly.

'I'm going to be thirty, single and homeless.' She drops her head into her hands and lets out a small sob. 'My life is a mess.'

'No, you are going to be thirty, single and *fabulous*.' Taking her hand in mine, I flash her a wink. 'I promise.'

This year I'm going to put my
mistletoe in my back pocket,
so everyone can kiss my ass...

December 3rd

Swiping a finger across the screen of my Kindle lazily, I stretch out my legs on the sofa. Sunday really is my favourite day of the week. The only day in the calendar when it is socially acceptable to do absolutely nothing from the moment you peel open your eyes, to the second that you crawl back under the duvet at night. Attempting to block out the rather comical loud bangs that are coming from the spare room, I try to lose myself in my latest chick lit download. My eyes scan the text as I curl up into a ball. I am contemplating opening a tin of Roses to silence my growling stomach when I hear Oliver's muffled voice calling out my name. Begrudgingly putting down my Kindle, I push myself to my feet and pad across the carpet in search of my husband.

After a little searching, I push open the door to the spare room to reveal Oliver balancing the world's biggest Christmas tree over his shoulder. My face breaks into a smile as I take in the scene in front of me. A selection of sparkly baubles and tinsel are scattered across the bed and a mountain of tangled fairy lights completely cover the carpet. Oliver is red in the face as he pushes the tree out of the doorway and lets it fall onto the living room floor with a clatter.

'That is a *lot* heavier than it looks.' Collapsing into an armchair, he tries to get his breath back.

'I know. It took four delivery men to carry it into the apartment, *remember*?' I squeeze onto the chair beside him and rest my head on his chest.

He nods in agreement and motions towards the huge floor to ceiling windows. 'This year, I say we put it right there.'

'Perfect!' Letting out an excited squeak, I plant a kiss on his nose before running into the kitchen. 'I'll get the Baileys, you get the decorations!'

As Oliver drags box after box of Christmas paraphernalia out of the spare room, I pour out two rather large measures of the calorific, creamy alcohol. Popping a couple of ice cubes into each glass, I place them down on the coffee table and wander off in search of my iPod. Last year, Oliver and I started our own Christmas tradition of decorating the tree with help of a bucket load of Baileys. This was then followed by a lot of drunken dancing to a mega Christmas mashup. Yes, we are quite clearly embarrassing parents in the making.

After digging my iPod out of the depths of my seemingly bottomless handbag, I hit play and pop it into the docking station. Within seconds, the iconic tones of Mariah Carey fill the room and I get a tingle of excitement in the pit of my stomach. Bending down to help Oliver separate the branches of the tree, I sing along to the music merrily. It took me ages to convince Oliver that we didn't *have* to have a real Christmas tree. When I was a child, the one and only time that we had a real tree my mother spent the whole of December on her hands and knees plucking pine needles out of the carpet. Since then, she successfully brainwashed my father and I into believing that artificial Christmas trees are the far superior option.

Thinking back to that time in my life makes me realise just how much my mother has changed. Until last year, my mother was extremely proud to be the UK's answer to Martha Stewart. A self-confessed homemaker, she exclusively wore twinsets and the only acrylics that she had were in the form of Tupperware boxes. To be honest, I hardly recognise the person that she is today. A matter of days after meeting Oliver's audacious mother, she was transformed into a bronzed, mini skirt wearing pussycat. Don't ask me how as I really, *really* do not know.

I watch Oliver drape tinsel over the tree clumsily and fight my perfectionist urge to straighten it out. Reaching into the box of decorations, I smile at the memory of purchasing them last year. Every bauble is either red or gold and each one sparkles manically under the bright spotlights. It took us at least two hours to make a decision on which ones to go for. With Oliver wanting purple and me longing for the more traditional colours, it took a lot of rock-paper-scissors to help us settle the argument.

Taking a seat on the floor, I dig through the box and pull out my favourite piece. Buried beneath a bag of tinsel is our wedding gift from Marc and Gina. Taking care not to drop it, I gently slide the beautiful decoration out of its velvet gift bag. The delicate bauble is made from the finest Swarovski crystal and the glitter that is floating around inside glistens wildly as I turn it over in my hands. Amazingly, the time and date of our wedding have been engraved into the surface. Of all the stunning gifts that we received, this is my favourite.

Pushing myself to my feet, I slide the loop of the bauble onto a branch and take a step back to admire it. Beneath the bright lights of the Christmas tree it glistens wildly, like the brightest star in the sky at night. Oliver passes me my drink and we clink our glasses together merrily. Christmas is coming and I for one cannot wait...

I'm terribly sorry that my OCD made decorating the Christmas tree a positively unpleasant experience...

December 4th

Arriving back at my desk after lunch, I take a sip of water and try to shake the growing nausea in my stomach. When did I become such a lightweight? I only had one pathetic glass of Baileys last night and I still awoke this morning feeling like I had done ten rounds with Mike Tyson. Convincing myself that it must have been Oliver's dodgy American bacon that has made me feel a little queasy, I drop my bag to the floor and flick on my computer. With it being so close to Christmas, there actually isn't *that* much for me to do. With Oliver finalising the spring collection down in the studio, Marc has moved me back to the seventh floor to *help aid client relations.* What this really means is that Marc's PA is on annual leave and he hasn't bothered to respond to an email in weeks. His blatant refusal to deal with his own correspondence has resulted in over a thousand unread emails and one too many disgruntled customers.

Sifting through the masses of junk mail, I have a quick scan around the office. I have actually really missed this place. Before Oliver joined the company, this was my designated floor. It was only when I was selected to assist him down in the studio that I had to move. Not that I was complaining, working with the gorgeous American that is now my husband was how my fairytale started. Lianna catches me staring into space and sticks out her tongue in concentration as she types. Laughing at her daftness, I turn my attention back to my own work. I actually have a lot thank Suave for. Not only has it made my dream of working in the fashion industry come true, it has also given me my two best friends *and* my hubby.

As I think about just how fortunate I have been, I watch a young intern try and fail to drape a flimsy piece of thinning tinsel around the vending machine. Offering her a friendly smile, I grab the singing Santa off the photocopier and sit him in the corner of my desk. This place could really do with a splash of festive cheer. Apart from the intern's sorry looking tinsel and my stolen Santa, there isn't so much as a glimpse of anything else Christmas related in the entire building. Determined to change this, I lock my computer screen and walk over to Marc's office. Knocking on the door gently, I let myself in when I see that he is alone.

'Hi!' I smile as I collapse into a plush

leather chair. 'You look *fantastic* today. New haircut?'

Marc scrunches up his nose suspiciously and puts his feet up on the desk. 'What the hell do you want?'

'Nothing! Can't I give one of my dearest friends a compliment without wanting anything in return?' I bat my eyelashes innocently as I twirl a strand of dark hair around my finger.

'You've got five seconds before I'm going into a meeting.' Marc checks his watch and holds up five fingers. 'Five.... four.... three...'

'OK!' I yell, leaning forward onto his desk. 'Can we have some Christmas decorations for the office?'

'The office is already decorated.' He fires back, not missing a beat.

'Are you kidding me? A flimsy piece of tinsel and a decade old singing Santa Clause do *not* count as decorations.'

'I don't know.' He replies slowly, rubbing his face.

'Oh, come on!' I push his feet off the desk playfully. 'Don't be such a Scrooge.'

He frowns for a moment before holding up his hands to surrender. 'Fine. You win.'

'Really?' I let out an excited squeal and clap my hands together.

'Yes. I will sort something out this week.

Now get out of here, I've got work to do.'
He flashes me a wink and motions towards
the door.

'Thank you! Thank you! Thank you!' I
blow him a kiss before skipping back over
to my desk.

I can't wait to get my hands on the
goodies and transform this grey office
block into a festive wonderland. Being
BFF's with the boss really does have its
perks sometimes. Unlocking my computer
screen, I imagine myself tossing glitter
over the worktops like a happy Christmas
elf. I can see it already. Spray-on snow for
the windows, a sprig of mistletoe for the
staff room, maybe I could push him into
getting a Christmas tree! I could even
dress up as Santa whilst I decorate. Just
call me, *the junior designer who saved
Christmas.*

Turning my attention back to Marc's
mountain of emails, I tap out an apologetic
response to an angry supplier who is
chasing up an unpaid invoice. Rebecca has
been away for all of five days and already
Marc is falling behind. I suddenly have a
worrying vision of the entire office falling
into chaos whilst Marc suns himself on
Bondi Beach. Personally, I don't think I
would like to be in a hot country for
Christmas. Wrapping up warm, sipping

mulled wine and praying for snow are all part of what make this time of year so magical. Although the idea of catching some rays whilst sipping an ice-cold beer *does* make me a little envious. Just don't tell Father Christmas... or his elves.

Anyone who believes that men are the equal of women has never seen a man trying to wrap a Christmas present.

December 5th

Clutching a box of Christmas crackers to my chest for dear life, I squeeze my way along the crowded Christmas aisle and back to the safety of Oliver. Considering that it is so early in the season, these shoppers are crazy! As we continue to work our way around the busy supermarket, I attempt to regain control of our wayward trolley. For the past twenty minutes, Oliver has been happily plucking a variety of yummy food off the shelves and tossing them in without a second thought. We are only on the third aisle and already our trolley is over-flowing.

Trying to resist the huge cupcake display that is screaming out at me, I leave Oliver salivating over the desserts and make my way over to the meat section. My stomach rumbles as I scan the rows of beef, chicken and lamb greedily. I can't help but laugh as a couple rows over which turkey crown to buy. Their argument is getting rather heated now, with the young man putting a piece of meat in their basket just for his lady friend to remove it immediately. I am still giggling to myself when a thought suddenly hits me. *One of us is going to have cook Christmas dinner!* Neither Oliver nor I have *any* cooking skills to write home about. My speciality is a baked potato with grated cheese and the most time that Oliver spends in the kitchen is to grab a takeout menu. I suddenly have an awful image of the seven of us sat around the table with a selection of pizza boxes. Oh, God! Just as I am about to have an almighty panic attack, Oliver appears in front of me with a pile of doughnuts.

'We have got *five* guests coming for Christmas and neither one of us can cook.' My voice is high and flustered, but Oliver just stares at me blankly. 'What are we going to do?'

'Don't worry about it.' He turns his attention to the beef medallions and shrugs his shoulders casually. 'We will figure something out and if we don't, there's always takeout.'

'*Oliver!*' I hit him on the arm with the pack of doughnuts. 'We can't have guests over for Christmas and serve them *pizza* or... or chicken tikka massala!'

He lets out a little laugh at my hysteria and continues throwing things into the trolley. 'Why not?'

'Because it's *Christmas*!' I throw my arms in the air and ignore the stares of passers-by. 'Christmas is about turkey with all the trimmings, roast potatoes and

Brussels sprouts! Over my dead body are we serving up junk food on Christmas day.'

'Then I'll cook.' Taking control of the trolley, he heads towards the bread.

'You?' I crinkle up my nose at the thought.

'Yeah.' He tosses me a seeded loaf and winks cheekily. 'Happy now?'

I nod in response, but I can't help feeling a little concerned. In all the time that I have known Oliver, the most he has ever cooked for me is a fry up in the morning and even that can be hit and miss. Running after him, I try to convince myself that everything will be all right. If he thinks he can handle it, then I have every faith in him. After all, cooking Christmas dinner for your in-laws and audacious, carb free, vegetarian mother sounds like a breeze, doesn't it?

* * *

Dropping our bags onto the dining table, we shed our wet coats and run to the radiator for warmth. To say that the weather outside is terrible would be an understatement. I lock eyes with Oliver and we both burst into a fit of giggles. Our wind battered hair, rain-soaked clothing and red noses look frankly comical. It's not even 6.30pm yet, but it has been dark for hours already. The heavy rain and strong winds combined with the dense darkness make it almost unbearable to stay outside for very long. I wander over to the floor to ceiling windows and look down at the busy streets below. The bright lights on the Christmas tree sparkle like crazy against the black night sky as hordes of people run along the pavement with umbrellas, desperate to find shelter from the wind and rain. Before I give in to the lure of the couch and a hot chocolate, I return to the kitchen to help Oliver with the food shopping. Filling the fridge with delicious cheeses and wine, I am soon distracted by a knocking at the door. Motioning for Oliver to answer it, I carry on unloading the shopping bags.

'Umm, Clara?' Oliver beckons me over to the doorway. 'You've got a visitor.'

'Who is it?' Wiping my hands on my jeans, I pop my head around the door. 'Lianna!' It takes me a moment to realise that she is carrying a rather large holdall. 'What... are you doing here?'

'My mum kicked me out.' Her brow creases in annoyance. 'Can I stay here for the night?'

'Sure.' I look at Oliver who nods in agreement and beckons her inside. 'Drink?'

'Absolutely!' Li replies, propping herself up at the breakfast bar.

I take a seat next to her and lower my voice so that Oliver can't hear. 'What the hell happened?'

'Nothing!' She holds up her hands to protest her innocence, but I can tell that she is lying. 'It's my mum! She is *so* dramatic!'

I squint my eyes at her suspiciously. 'She wouldn't kick you out for nothing, Li. Tell me what happened.'

Oliver places two cold beers on the counter in front of us and disappears into the living room. Bless him. I have trained him well.

Taking a big slug of her drink, Li lets out a sigh. 'It's Martin. My mum *hates* him.'

'Martin?' I run my fingers over the cold bottle and scrunch up my nose in confusion.

'Martin.' She repeats. 'Their neighbour's son.'

'OK...' I reply slowly. 'What does their neighbour's son have to do with you?'

'I bumped into him last night on my way home from work and he asked me out for a drink.' She shrugs her shoulders and pulls a packet of crisps out of one of the shopping bags.

'And then?' I probe, not willing to drop

the conversation so easily.

'And then... I invited him in for coffee.' Looking away in embarrassment, she shoves a handful of crisps into her mouth.

'Lianna!' I yell, unable to keep my voice down.

'What?' Her cheeks turn pink as she jumps on the defensive.

'You can't keep bringing guys back to your parent's house!' My head throbs as I start to wonder if she has lost her mind. 'No wonder they are annoyed with you.'

'I know. That is why I need to get my own place.'

'No. You can't keep bringing back guys full stop.' Rubbing my temples, I let out a heavy sigh. 'You don't need to be with a man to be happy, you know that.'

'That's easy for you to say, you've got Oliver to cuddle up to at night.' She turns to face me and I notice that her eyes are filled with tears.

'Come here.' I hold out my arms and she rests her head on my shoulder.

As her tears soak my jumper, I stroke her hair gently. I don't know whether this is a mid-life crisis due to her impending birthday or a delayed reaction to the collapse of her relationship with Dan. Either way, I need to find a way to pull her out this depression and with Christmas just around the corner, I need to find one fast.

Dear Santa,
It was all Lianna's fault...

December 6th

Digging through the bags of tinsel, I hand Lianna a pile of metallic baubles and get to work at untangling a string of pink fairy lights. As promised, Marc dumped a mountain of decorations on my desk first thing this morning and ever since I have been just itching to get my hands on them. Surprisingly, he actually *did* get us a Christmas tree. Granted it is only two feet tall and a little sparse, but now that we have loaded it up with bling it actually looks pretty good.

Letting out a little yawn, I check my watch for the tenth time today. We still have just over two hours to go and I am already absolutely exhausted. It was almost daylight when I finally crawled into bed last night. After Lianna appeared at our apartment yesterday, we spent the rest of the night drawing up a plan to get her life back on track. For a good few hours, she was adamant that a one-way ticket to Barbados was the only option. However, with a little encouragement and the help of a few Desperados she eventually agreed not to leave the country.

After a lot of conferring, Oliver and I

decided that Li was going to stay with us for a couple of weeks until she manages to find herself somewhere to live. She has promised to stay away from men *and* women for that matter and is going to put all her efforts into building herself a future. I keep reminding her that if you aren't happy with yourself being single, chances are you won't be happy with yourself in a relationship either. As my mother always said, you have to learn to fall in love with yourself before the rest of the world will fall in love with you, too.

'Did you manage to call around any of those property rentals we found?' I ask, trying to keep my voice light and airy.

'I did.' She flashes me a small smile and grabs a chair to hammer a piece of mistletoe to the ceiling. 'I'm actually going to view one this weekend.'

'Fantastic! I reply encouragingly. 'What is it? Apartment? House?'

'It's a semi in Bakersfield.' Hammering a drawing pin into the ceiling, she tucks a stray strand of hair behind her ear. 'Two bedrooms, small conservatory. It needs a little work, a lick of paint here and there, but nothing major.'

'How do you feel about it being in Bakersfield?' I ask, pursing my lips.

Bakersfield is an up and coming town

around thirty minutes from our apartment. In the past, it *did* get a little bit of bad press when the university first opened due to the student takeover, but property developers recently tried to revamp the area.

'I don't mind Bakersfield.' Li mumbles. 'Pablo and I spent a lot of time there.'

Oh, no. She said the *P*-word.

Not wanting to make eye contact with her, I turn my attention to the fairy lights. 'Have you heard anything from Pablo since he left?'

She shakes her head in response and dives back into the box of decorations. Not wanting to push the subject, I decide not to say anything more about him. It was immediately after she broke up with Dan that Lianna met Pablo. During a whirlwind two days in Tenerife, Li declared that Pablo was the love of her life and brought him back to the UK with her. It's fair to say that Pablo was a holiday romance that came just at the right time. Unfortunately, when the harsh reality of the real world hit home, things fizzled out and Pablo returned home to Tenerife.

'I did hear from Dan though...'

'What?' I exclaim. Did she just say, *Dan?* 'Dan?'

'Yep.' She replies breezily.

'What the hell did he want?' My heart pounds as I dread to think what she is going to say next.

'He asked for his engagement ring back.'

My mouth falls open as I stare at her in shock. That's low a blow even for a scumbag like Dan. 'What did you tell him?' I ask, trying to keep my voice low.

She turns to face me and a wicked smile plays at the corners of her mouth. 'I told him that I flushed it down the toilet.'

'You didn't!' I laugh.

'Of course, I didn't. I pawned it, but he doesn't need to know that.'

We both burst into a fit of giggles and try to compose ourselves as Marc steps into the office.

'All right you two, that's enough with the decorations. It's like Santa's grotto in here.' He looks up at the mistletoe and shakes his head.

'What's rattled your cage?' Li drapes a piece of tinsel around his neck and sprinkles him with glitter.

'Nothing!' He scowls, brushing gold glitter off the sleeve of his jacket.

'Oh, come on! We haven't even got the lights up yet.' Waving the string of pink lights around to emphasise my point, I stick out my bottom lip.

'I said enough!' He yells over his

shoulder as he marches to his office.

I wait for him to slam the office door before pushing myself to my feet. 'Right, where should we hang these lights?'

When you stop believing in Santa, you get socks for Christmas...

December 7th

For many years now, Marc, Lianna and I
have made an annual trip to the Christmas
markets in Greenton. This one night a year
enables us to drink our weight in mulled
wine and buy expensive quirky gifts that no
one really wants. That is why on a cold
Thursday night we find ourselves huddled
around an electric heater and working our
way through the drinks menu. Well, I say
we, but what I really mean is, everyone
except me. Marc and Oliver are happily
glugging away at a strange looking ale,
while Li and Gina are on their fourth mug
of potent Gluhwein. Sugar plus alcohol is
not a good combination for Gina. The extra
energy has meant that she hasn't stopped
talking for the past two hours.

Taking a sip of the hot mulled wine, I
grimace at the taste and pretend to listen
as Gina reels off her plans for Australia.
Normally I love drinking mulled wine at the
Christmas markets, but this year it just
tastes like stale dishwater. When I was
growing up, I thought that my dad was
insane for eating blue cheese. He would
insist that my taste buds would change as I
got older, but I never believed him. I guess

now that I am approaching thirty he is finally proving me wrong. Maybe I will have to give Gorgonzola another go. I always did wonder what it was that made people go weak at the knees at the sight of a mouldy piece of dairy.

Not feeling in the mood for drinking, I place my mug on the table and rub my hands together for warmth. This has to be a contender for the coldest December on record. It has snowed heavily on and off for the past week, whereas last year we only got snow once and even that was more slush than snow. I *knew* that global warming was a load of codswallop. Realising that Gina has now turned her attention to Lianna, I spy my chance to escape. To be honest, it is so incredibly busy in here that I don't even think they will notice.

Zipping up my coat, I squeeze through the sea of people and let my nose lead me to the stalls of yummy food. I watch in amusement as a stressed-out mother exchanges a fistful of notes for a bag of festive gingerbread men. The three children who are jumping around by her side squeal with delight as she dishes out the tasty treats. Reminding myself that I don't particularly like gingerbread, I smile at the flustered woman and carry on walking.

The cold air bites at my exposed nose as I stop to look at a busy stall. The vendor smiles eagerly, mentally ordering me to make a purchase. Rows and rows of tiny jars line the table top, each one decorated with glitter and Christmas tree gems. I reach down and gently turn over the labels. *Chilli Marmalade, Rum and Raisin Chocolate Spread, Hazelnut and Nutmeg Syrup.* They all sound amazing! Picking up one of each, I pay the pretty stall holder and pop the small bag into my pocket.

Trying not to give in to the huge Frankfurter sausages, I promise myself that I will most definitely visit Bavaria next year. It is the one place on my bucket list that is so near, yet once the Christmas hype dies down I completely forget how much I want to go. Oliver would love it, too. The amazing artwork, the unique gifts, the sweet temptations and the handcrafted woodwork. He would love it all. Making a mental note to look into it, I push my way through crowd.

I might be a good few stalls away, but I can hear Gina's ridiculously loud cackle as though she is stood right next to me. Glad that they haven't noticed I have gone, I nod my head in time to the music and trudge through the snow. I really want to get Oliver something for Christmas whilst I am here. Scanning the various stalls, I can't find anything that seems appropriate. Last year we decided not to do gifts and instead booked a weekend away in Chester. I was actually mortified when Oliver surprised me with a stunning pair of diamond earrings on Christmas morning and promised myself that next year I would get him the best gift ever. Just what *is* the best gift ever? That is the question.

Light snowflakes fall from the sky as I watch a group of young girls sprint into McDonald's for shelter. The youngest of the three screams loudly and tugs her Christmas jumper up over her head. Laughing quietly, I try to remember what it was like to have my biggest worry being getting my hair wet. Men don't seem to realise just what a disaster it is to have three hours of straightening ruined in seconds by a quick rain shower. With a splash of water, my hair can go from Jennifer Aniston to Edward Scissorhands in ten seconds flat.

My eyes land on a stunning snow globe that is glistening under the bright lights of the stall. Removing a mitten to pick it up, I give it a shake and watch as the snow sparkles inside the glass. In the centre, a beautiful Christmas tree is dressed in baubles which shine like rubies as the glitter swirls around the branches. I suddenly have an overwhelming longing to step inside and lose myself in the wintry scene. Deciding that I *have* to have it, I join the queue and dig around for my purse. I watch in fascination as the market trader wraps the delicate ornament in sheets of embossed paper. Yes, it might be expensive, but if you can't treat yourself at Christmas, when can you?

Clutching my new purchase carefully, I suddenly feel a little guilty. I am supposed to be buying gifts for other people, not myself. So far, I have treated myself to three lovely condiments and now an amazing snow globe that I don't have any place for and most certainly didn't need. Reminding myself that Christmas is about giving, I decide that these will all be stocking fillers, who for I really don't know. Christmas would be a hell of a lot easier if we all bought gifts for ourselves instead. No unwanted M&S vouchers from Auntie Patricia, no wrestling other customers for the last of the gift sets in Boots and certainly no worrying about what it is that people really want. For months on end, I have been racking my brains for the perfect gift to get for Oliver. Something that will take his breath away, something that he will appreciate and something that he doesn't already have. Well, if all else fails, I'm pretty sure that he doesn't have any Hazelnut and Nutmeg Syrup...

It just isn't Christmas unless you push your body to the brink of alcoholism and diabetes...

December 8ᵗʰ

Stopping for breath, I peer into the pram and feel an incredible rush of adrenaline as I see that MJ has finally fallen asleep. This is *not* part of my job description. How I have gone from designing shoes to running a crèche, I really do not know. How do women *do* this every day? I feel like I have run a bloody marathon. My feet are aching and my arms feel like lead. Removing my scarf, I take a seat outside Starbucks and try to regain some feeling in my toes. The temperature might be near freezing, but it is safe to say that I am absolutely melting.

Catching a glimpse of my reflection in the window, I let out a little laugh. My face is red and my eyes are puffy from all the panting. I have only been doing this for an hour and already I look like a victim of Japanese water torture. No wonder Gina has lost so much weight since having the kids. Pushing eighteen pounds of baby around is not as easy as it looks. Looking to my left, I watch as a young mother pushes a twin buggy effortlessly along the pavement. Two toddlers dressed in matching Christmas jumpers are walking happily by her side. She looks like she has just stepped off a Mamas and Papas advert. She shoots me a smug smile as she passes by and coos at the adorable twin boys that are laughing blissfully from their designer pram. My eyes fall to her ridiculously high heels and I let out a quiet gasp. How is she *doing* that?

Hoping that my skin hasn't turned green with envy, I dig my phone out of my pocket and check my emails. Still nothing from Marc. He *promised* that he wouldn't be longer than half an hour, but that was almost two hours ago! Normally I would never offer to be the babysitter, but Marc was so stressed-out earlier that I didn't have the heart to say no. Unbelievably, he decided to book the tickets for Australia without getting MJ a passport first. This resulted in a frantic Gina flying off to the Passport Office and with Marc in an important business meeting, it was down to Lianna and I to take charge of the children. Annoyingly, I most *definitely* got the short straw. I'm guessing that entertaining Madison is a whole lot easier than trying to get a cranky three-month-old to sleep.

Pushing myself to my feet, I wipe my sweaty brow and head back towards the office. Considering that it is lunch-time, the streets are fairly quiet. A quick look into the adjacent shopping centre tells me exactly where all the people are. Grateful not to be caught up in the hustle and bustle of the Christmas shoppers, I watch MJ smiling in his sleep as I walk. When he isn't crying, he is absolutely adorable. His chubby pink cheeks and tiny button nose make him ridiculously cute. Unlike Madison, MJ looks nothing like Marc or Gina. He almost reminds me of a little Cabbage Patch doll although I would *never* admit that to his parents.

A flashing sign in a shop window informs me that there are just eighteen days until Christmas. That gives me little over two weeks to get myself sorted. My stomach does a little flip as I draw up a mental to-do list. With Lianna's 30th birthday being just days away and Oliver's parents arriving from Texas next Wednesday, I have more than enough on my plate. I still have to purchase a bunch of gifts and I have absolutely no idea when my own parents are arriving.

Trying not to panic at the dawning realisation of just how much I have got to do, I take a deep breath and wait for the green man before crossing the street. Whoever said that moving house, getting married and having a baby are the three most stressful things that you will ever do, obviously never hosted Christmas for their in-laws.

∗   ∗   ∗

'What a day!' I exclaim, clinking my glass against Lianna's. 'Who knew that child minding was so stressful?'

'Tell me about it.' Li replies, taking a big slug of Rioja. 'That child should come with a warning.'

'Oh, come off it! You know that I got the short straw. Try pushing MJ around town for two hours in the freezing cold whilst he screams like a broken blender.' My head begins to throb at the recollection of his ear-piercing squeals.

Lianna laughs and shakes her head before diving into her handbag and producing her beloved Chanel lipstick. '*This* was the best part of thirty quid.'

Passing me the offending article, she stretches her legs out on the couch and waits for my reaction. The glossy black container is sticky and covered in grubby little fingerprints. I brace myself before pulling off the lid. Uh, oh. The tip has been ground down to a blunt stub and it has been dipped in what looks suspiciously like chocolate.

'What the hell happened to it?' I drop the

lipstick onto the coffee table and wipe my hands on my jeans.

'Madison. Madison happened to it.' Li screws up her nose and kicks off her shoes. 'I swear, I am never having kids. *Ever*.'

'I don't think that *all* children will destroy your high-end beauty products.' I reach down for the wine bottle and refill our glasses.

'Either way, I don't fancy going through hours of agony only to be rewarded with something that screams all day and pukes all night.' Shuddering at the thought, she dives into the bowl of nachos and turns up the television.

'Hmm.' I reply, not really agreeing with her.

There must be *something* about having children that women of our age find so appealing. As I am pondering what it is about babies that make females want to go to hell and back to get one, my thought bubble is burst by Lianna's tipsy voice.

'Plus, you can't drink wine for nine months.'

The thought of going wine free for almost a year makes me want to have my tubes tied immediately. 'Good point.'

'Refill?' She asks, waving around the half empty bottle.

'Most definitely.'

I am trying to get into the Christmas spirit... but the damn bottle just won't open!

December 9th

Today is going to be a good day. That is what I told myself when I rolled out of bed this morning, but with each hour that passes, I have been proven to be very, *very* wrong. From splashing bleach in my hair whilst cleaning the bathroom to running out of petrol on the way to Lianna's house viewing - it's safe to say that today hasn't gotten off to the best start. Now that we have eventually been refuelled and had a much-needed shot of caffeine, we are finally on our way.

'I don't know why we are even bothering.' Lianna grumbles from the back seat. 'If this morning is anything to go by then this house is *bound* to be a disaster.'

'Where's that positive attitude we talked about?' Oliver squints at her through his rear-view mirror and flashes her a wink.

Li mumbles something under her breath and we both pretend not to hear. Turning around to face her, I smile sympathetically. It's not just me that has had a bad day. With the hairdresser fully booked in the run up to Christmas, Li decided to give her fringe a quick trim herself. Needless to say, it didn't go very well. Her usually soft sweeping fringe has been hacked down to nothing more than a choppy stump at the side of her face. Trying not to laugh as she attempts to slick it back with a handful of bobby pins, I run my fingers through my own tangled mane. With my spontaneous blonde streak and her disastrous DIY job, we must look a right pair.

I really hope that this house is what she is looking for. Although I have to admit that I'm not getting my hopes up. With her birthday drawing ever closer, it would make turning thirty a whole lot easier for her knowing that she doesn't have to sofa surf anymore. With Oliver and I being happily married, it makes seeing Lianna hit rock bottom even harder. I almost feel guilty for having my own life in order whilst hers falls spectacularly apart. On a brighter note, Marc and Gina are planning a surprise birthday party for her before they leave for Australia! I haven't told Oliver yet as I don't want to be worried about him letting the cat out of the bag. Normally I share everything with my husband, but there is no way that he would able to keep this one a secret. I'm finding it difficult myself to be honest.

Turning up the heaters in an attempt to warm up my cold hands, I watch slightly mesmerised as tiny snowflakes land on the windscreen. One good thing about today is that we have Oliver with us. Driving in the snow has always made me feel a little anxious, so when he offered to be our chauffeur I jumped at the chance. The plan is to check out Lianna's potential new pad and then hit the shops to get our Christmas gifts sorted. As usual, it didn't take more than the promise of a little retail therapy for me to sign up, although Oliver's intentions were a little less selfish.

'Thanks for doing this.' I whisper, giving his knee a gentle squeeze.

I know that traipsing around the shops with two women is Oliver's idea of hell, so I really appreciate him giving up his golfing weekend to help us out. Little does he know that I don't intend on going home until I have bought each and every present on my list. Given that my list isn't exactly short and sweet, I think it's best that I keep that last part to myself, at least for now anyway...

* * *

She *has* to like this place, it's almost impossible not to. I glance at Oliver who is braving the cold to explore the gardens and nodding appreciatively. After a morning from hell, none of us were expecting much from this property, but it's actually pretty big and the interior isn't that bad at all. Yes, it needs a little TLC, a lick of paint here and there, but what property doesn't? I run my hand over the ornate fireplace and try to imagine this place dressed up for Christmas. I picture a huge tree in the bay window with twinkling fairy lights and greeting cards on every surface. This is the one, I know it. Hearing Lianna coming down the stairs with the estate agent, I try to get the gist of their conversation.

'Clara?' Li smiles broadly and motions outside. 'Can I talk to you for a moment?'

I nod in response and zip up my coat before following her to the back door.

'Well?' I ask, the second that we are out of earshot.

'I love it!' She smiles, her eyes sparkling as she takes a step back and looks up at the house. 'I think it's pretty much perfect.'

'This is so exciting!' I clap my hands together excitedly and pull up my hood to protect my ears from the wind. 'When can you move in?'

'The house has been empty for almost a month so I can move in right away.'

'Yay!' I let out a squeal and pull her in for a hug. 'See, I told you that the best things happen when you least expect it.'

'You did.' She agrees as we make our way back inside. 'And the best part is that the owner ultimately wants to sell the property. They have offered me a twelve-month lease to test the place out with a view to buy next year.'

'That's fantastic!' I squeal. 'It must be fate.'

'What is?' Oliver interjects, appearing from the conservatory.

I let Lianna fill him in on the good news and smile as he gives her a celebratory high five. Nothing makes me happier than seeing two of my favourite people laughing and joking. Well, apart from cocktails and food. My stomach rumbles loudly and I suddenly realise that in the chaos of this morning we haven't eaten a thing all day.

'It looks like we're getting our spare room back.' I announce, as Li skips off to sign the lease. 'I think this calls for a celebration!'

'Does this mean that we can forget about the shopping?' Oliver's eyes glint hopefully as he looks down at his watch.

'Not a chance...'

* * *

Stumbling out of the crowded shopping centre clutching a mountain of carrier bags, I look down at my shopping list and breathe a sigh of relief. After five hours of epic retail therapy, I have *finally* crossed almost every name off my list. Feeling pretty satisfied that our hard work has paid off, I rub my cold nose and bury my chin into my scarf. I think it is safe to say that today has been a massive success after all. Glancing at Lianna, a slight smile plays on the corner of my lips as I listen to her discussing interior design options with Oliver. Oh, I do love it when a plan comes together.

Glancing at my watch, I am shocked to see that it is almost 9.00pm. If I don't eat soon, I think I am going to pass out. Running around a manic shopping centre in sub-zero temperatures on an empty stomach is *not* a good idea. On the plus side, being slightly delirious from hunger has made making snap decisions on gifts a whole lot easier. My usual procrastination over even the smallest purchase has been replaced with a manic snatch and grab manoeuvre, which sees me throwing items into my basket without a second thought of the price. God help my bank balance.

'I think I am all shopped out.' Lianna yawns loudly as a flustered woman pulls down the shutters to a department store.

'Thank God!' Oliver sighs, rolling his

eyes. 'Christmas is supposed to be the season to be jolly, *not* the season to be subjected to torture.'

'Don't be so dramatic.' Playfully punching him in the arm, I motion towards a Mexican eatery and bite my lip hopefully. 'I don't suppose anyone's hungry?'

Thankfully, I don't even need to wait for them to answer. The second those words escape my lips they immediately start running towards the restaurant. Not wanting to risk falling on the icy road, I shake my head and tread carefully across the snow. By the time that I have pushed my way inside, Oliver and Li have secured a cosy booth at the back of the busy restaurant. Shaking off my coat and mittens, I dump my bags under the table and reach for the menu. Luckily, Lianna has already taken the liberty of ordering a round bubbles. Unfortunately for Oliver, the only bubbles he will be having are those in his Pepsi. My stomach grumbles as I eye up the menu and order a full three courses. Convincing myself that I will start the diet tomorrow, I kick back in my seat and dive into the complimentary nachos. My fingers are like icicles as I dunk a nacho into a huge mound of sour cream.

The waitress places our drinks down on the table and Oliver immediately proposes a toast. 'To our dear friend, Lianna. May 2016 be your best year yet.' He flashes her a wink and holds out his Pepsi.

'To Lianna.' I echo, raising my glass and clinking it against theirs.

Li's cheeks turn a deep shade of pink as she takes a sip of the frosty bubbles and smiles in embarrassment. Feeling a little sorry for Oliver and his measly pint of Pepsi, I switch our glasses around and inform him that I will be the designated driver for the night. It hardly seems fair that we have dragged him around the shops and now we are going to drink yummy cocktails in front of him. Lianna's eyes glisten with excitement as she pulls out her house brochure and proceeds to flips through the pages. At last, I can start to relax and enjoy the festivities. Lianna is finally getting back on her feet and I have pretty much done with my Christmas gifts. Feeling quite pleased with myself, I pull off my scarf and turn to face Lianna when Oliver's phone vibrates on the table.

'Excuse me.' Picking up the handset, Oliver squeezes his way through the loud restaurant, leaving Lianna and I alone.

'I'm *so* relieved that you have found somewhere to live.' I flash her a bright smile and take a sip of my drink.

'Why? Were you and Oliver going to

throw me out, too?' She laughs and sticks out her tongue, but I know that she is only half joking. 'Seriously, thanks for having me these past few days. It really means a lot to me that you guys put up with me when no one else will.'

Taking her hand in mine, I feel a lump form in my throat. 'You don't need to thank us. I know that you would do the same for me.'

'Well, I don't know about that. If I had to spend another night listening to your snoring I think I would have to kill you.'

'*What?*' I retort. 'I think you will find that the snoring is *not* me.'

Lianna raises her eyebrows and shoots Oliver a smile as he slides back into the booth next to her. 'Everything OK?'

I can tell by the look on his face that everything is not OK. I can also tell by the light dusting of powder on his shoulders that it has started to snow again.

'Yeah...' He replies uncertainly.

'It's obviously not.' Laughing nervously, I play with the stem of my glass as he takes a deep breath.

'That was my mom. Well, actually it was *your* mom.'

'OK...' I catch Lianna's eye and she looks equally confused.

'Apparently, your parents are in Texas

and have been for the past two weeks.' He runs a hand through his long hair and laughs uneasily.

'What?' More confused than ever, I lean over the table to block out any background noise from the other diners. 'What the hell are my parents doing in Texas?'

'They have been visiting *my* parents.' Shaking his head in disbelief, he takes a swing of his drink. 'They got some last-minute flights to escape the cold and have been kicking back in the sun.'

The thought of my parents together with Oliver's unsupervised makes me feel queasy. Since my mum met Randy and Janie she has changed considerably. The once prim and proper Rosemary has been transformed into a mini skirt wearing Janie double act. Don't get me wrong, it's fantastic that they get along so well. It's just that I really don't want them coming back with tongue piercings and matching tattoos.

'Anyway...' Oliver's voice pierces my thought bubble. 'The reason that they were calling is that they are all arriving together. The formidable foursome will be with us on Wednesday evening.'

My stomach churns as I try to process what he has just said. Both of our parents arriving together. That means double trouble. I had come to terms with Janie and Randy coming this week, but my own parents weren't meant to be arriving until Christmas Eve. Exhaling loudly, I bite the end of my straw. It's universally accepted that when one area of your life comes together, the world throws you yet another curveball. Yes, that might sound a little dramatic, but you haven't met my parents *or* my in-laws...

Christmas is all about having your entire dysfunctional family under one roof and hoping that no one gets arrested.

December 10th

Tugging at the sleeve of my flannel pyjamas, I close my laptop and slide under the duvet. I know that it is December and the weather is *supposed* to be cold, wet and rainy, but feeling like you are stepping into an igloo whenever you try to leave your bed is not normal. Hearing Lianna pad around in the spare room, I squeeze my eyes closed and snuggle into Oliver's back. Last night I foolishly agreed to accompany Li to IKEA this morning. Annoyingly, Oliver used his get out of jail free card to go to the gym with Marc. Why anyone would want to go to a gym two weeks before Christmas is beyond me. Christmas is the only time of the year when it is deemed acceptable to eat your weight in chocolate and drink before lunch. Exercise is the last thing on my mind during the festive season. Come to think of it, exercise is *always* the last thing on my mind.

Oliver suddenly stirs and lets out a low groan. His dark curls hang in front of his sleepy eyes as he stretches out his arms and lets out a huge yawn. 'Aren't you going furniture shopping with Li?'

'Don't remind me.' I roll my eyes and

stick out my bottom lip in protest. 'I have done enough shopping in these past few days to last a lifetime!'

'Just think, the sooner Lianna moves out, the sooner we get our apartment back.' Oliver's eyes glint wickedly as he nuzzles his chin into my neck.

Tearing myself out of his arms, I roll out of my bed and push myself to my feet. 'I think you will find that as soon as Lianna moves *out*, our parents move *in*.'

Ignoring Oliver's groans, I twist my ridiculously long hair up onto my head and try to stop my teeth from chattering. I desperately need a haircut. My usually bouncy, shoulder length curls are now trailing wildly down my back. Normally I would have chopped it off the second it crept past my collarbone, but with it being near freezing outside it acts like a hairy water bottle around my neckline. Yes, it really is *that* cold. Reaching for my favourite jumper, I quickly pull on my skinny jeans and make for the bathroom, leaving Oliver dozing on the bed.

The bathroom tiles are freezing under my feet as I load my toothbrush with minty paste. Catching a glimpse of my reflection in the mirror makes me shudder. Winter really is a killer for your skin. The golden glow that I spent so long achieving is nowhere to be seen. I would actually go as far as to say that my skin tone has bypassed porcelain and is now a rather worrying transparent shade. Dracula, eat your heart out.

Popping my toothbrush back into its holder, I splash some water on my face in an attempt to wake myself up. Lately, no matter how many hours sleep I get, I still wake up like an exhausted troll. Making a mental note to upgrade my anti-wrinkle cream, I flick off the bathroom light and collapse onto the bed with my cosmetic case. As Oliver snores gently, I set to work on bringing some life to my dreary face. Thank God for highlighter! I really do not know what I would do without the magical pen that is Touché Éclat.

Once suitably satisfied that I look more like a human and less like a poorly built snowman, I plant a kiss on Oliver's toasty cheek and wander into the living room. A trail of breadcrumbs across the carpet informs me that Lianna is alive and kicking. Following the mess into the kitchen, I shake my head at the state of what is usually a pristine work space. Empty cartons of milk are strewn across the work tops and a litter of chocolate wrappers have been poorly hidden under the Christmas tree. I do love Lianna, but her untidiness drives me insane. Grabbing an empty carrier bag, I begin to clear away the chaos that is the aftermath of a Lianna tornado.

This must be what having a child is like, I think to myself as I remove a dirty sock from the back of the couch. I remember how beautiful Marc's apartment looked before Madison and MJ arrived. These days, his luxury HD television screen is covered in sticky fingerprints and where his much-loved pool table once stood is a huge Donald Duck playpen. I can't help but think that people who have kids must be crazy. Picking up the offending article with the help of a chewed pen, I toss it into the washing machine and slam the door shut. She really is a pig.

Washing my hands and flicking on the coffee maker, I wander over to the Christmas tree and watch the baubles sparkle under the spotlights. Not long now, I think to myself, fiddling with a piece of tinsel. So much to do and just two short weeks to do it in. I have fifteen days to go and something tells me that I am going to need each and every one of them...

Christmas is cancelled.
Apparently, you told Santa that you had
been good this year... he died laughing.

December 11th

'Are you kidding?' I cross my arms and stare at Marc in disbelief. 'What if something gets damaged?' I glance over at Oliver who lets out a little chuckle. 'I'm being serious!'

'Clara, it's a Christmas party for a bunch of thirty-something women, not an all out rave in a mosh pit.' Marc rolls his eyes as he always does when he thinks that I am being dramatic.

'Erm... *thirty* something?' I raise my eyebrows accusingly. 'I think you will find that some of us are still in our *twenties*.' Smiling smugly, I flash Marc a cheeky wink.

Feeling rather pleased with myself at being the baby of the group, I fold my arms and sit back in my seat. Due to the huge budget cuts this year, the Suave Christmas party is being held right here in the office. Personally, I think plying people with alcohol and festive cheer around thousands of pounds worth of office equipment is a total recipe for disaster, but what do I know? With Marc and Gina flying out to Australia on the 22nd, the party is being held on the 20th. Five days after

Lianna's birthday and five days before Christmas day. Perfect timing. Now, if I could only get my head around our parents coming to stay and transform into Nigella Lawson to cook a traditional Christmas dinner for seven hungry people, everything would be A-OK.

As Marc fills Oliver in on his big Australian adventure, I try not to feel envious of him jetting off to the sun. Passport disaster aside, it sounds like they are going to have a fantastic time. It wasn't that long ago that Oliver was pushing for us to spend this Christmas across the pond, too. Being a Texas boy at heart, Oliver is used to sipping a beer in his cowboy boots and toasting marshmallows on an open fire. A little different to cradling a glass of Bailey's and a classic mince pie. It's not very often that the cultural differences come between us. Aside from the odd argument over him drenching my morning bacon in maple syrup, we actually get along really well.

Leaving the boys to talk, I slip out of Marc's office in search of Lianna. The entire floor is buzzing with festive cheer. Even the grumpy mail man is smiling. Noticing that her desk is empty, I am about to return to Marc's office when I spot her pushing her way through the sea of desks with a mountain of magazines. I can tell by her red nose that it must be below freezing outside. Not surprising considering that it is almost Christmas. A quick glance out of the window confirms my suspicions. It's not even 3.30pm and already the sky is a magical shade of black. It's hard to believe that in six short months we will be basking in sunshine way into the evening. Shaking my head to erase the image of gin cocktails and sunburnt shoulders, I turn my attention to my best friend.

'What have you got there?' I ask, snatching a magazine from the top of the pile. 'More interior design ideas?'

She nods in response and drops the huge pile onto the desk before collapsing into a chair. 'It is *manic* out there!' Rubbing her hands together for warmth, she listens carefully as I fill her in on Marc's Christmas party idea. 'Really?' She crinkles up her nose in confusion. 'What if something gets damaged?'

'That's exactly what I said.' Laughing, I perch on the edge of her desk and flip open Home Design UK. 'So, do you feel better about the big 3-0 now that you've got yourself a place sorted?'

'I really do.' She replies, fiddling with her Santa Clause earrings. 'I'm just hoping that I can get moved in before my birthday.'

'I'm sure that's doable.' I murmur, reminding myself that we will soon have an extra four pairs of hands to help.

'Are you ready for the in-laws arriving?' Lianna asks, as if reading my mind.

'Pretty much.' I respond, very aware that I haven't lifted a finger yet.

Every night I have promised myself that I will make a start on the guest bedrooms, but somehow I have found myself in a food coma on the sofa surrounded by empty chocolate wrappers. I blame Christmas. Christmas and its delicious foods and festive cheer. Promising myself that I will deal with it tonight, I slide off the desk.

'Just so you know, I'm staying out tonight.' Lianna offers me a small smile and flicks on her computer.

'Oh, God!' I let out a tired sigh and shoot her a disappointed look. 'I thought we had dealt with the whole *staying out* thing?'

'Not like that.' She fires back angrily. 'I'm staying at my new place tonight.'

'Oh... but you haven't moved anything in yet, have you?' I mumble, feeling a little bad for assuming the worst.

'That's kind of the whole point. Just me, my sleeping bag and a takeout pizza.' Blushing slightly, she tucks a stray strand of hair behind her ear. 'I'm christening my new pad Lianna style.'

Laughing at her craziness, I shake my head and make my way back to my desk. She might be a little bit weird, but Li will always be my best friend. My best friend who drinks too much, swears a lot and has very questionable morals. Catching her eye, I flash her a wink and smile widely. Lianna's back and I for one couldn't be happier about it.

*Do you know what I got for Christmas
last year?
Fat.
I got fat.*

December 12th

Crashing onto the couch on Tuesday evening, it takes me all of my will power not to fall into a much-needed sleep. If I wasn't extremely aware that we have visitors coming in twenty-four hours, I would be happily drooling into a cushion right now. This time tomorrow, we will have been invaded by four demanding pensioners and I haven't even made a *start* on my preparations. Letting out a huge groan, I roll off the bed and pad into the living room.

Today has been hectic, to say the least. Not only have I been busy replying to Marc's ridiculous backlog of emails, I have also been tasked with sorting the final details of Lianna's surprise birthday party. As far as Li is aware, Oliver and I are taking her for out a quiet meal at her favourite Indian restaurant. Little does she know that we are actually going to Snowflake - an uber cool, pop-up bar in the centre of town. For as long as I can remember, as soon as it hits December 1st, Snowflake appears outside the Town Hall. With its sparkly, silver interior and funky igloo shaped booths, it really is the place to be in the run-up to Christmas.

For years Li has begged us to go, but the queue of freezing people outside and extortionate entry prices has been more than enough to put us off. Realising that he got a fifty percent discount if he booked through Suave, Marc had the genius idea of hiring the place out for Lianna's birthday! So far, we have had almost a hundred people RSVP. I didn't even know that Li knew a hundred people. At least it won't be one of those dire parties where just ten pitiful guests try desperately to fill the dance floor. Let's face it, we've all been subjected to at least one. I can't wait to see her face when she realises what he has done. I am almost more excited about Lianna's party than I am about Christmas. Almost, but not quite.

Pouring myself a coffee, I grab a note pad and draw up a rather lengthy to-do list. Thankfully, Lianna is spending another night at her new place and with Oliver at the gym, I shouldn't have any distractions in getting things done. For the first time in a long time, I have absolutely no excuses. Clutching the steaming mug of energy, I slope into the guest bedroom and get to work tearing off the bedding. Deciding between floral prints and classic white takes me way longer than necessary. If only I had something red, green and covered in reindeers it would make this so much easier.

Half an hour later I collapse into a sweaty heap on the floor. Changing a bed shouldn't be this hard. Stupid Oliver and his ridiculous four poster beds. Why on Earth beds have to be this big, I really have no idea. Unless he is intending on inviting the local football team to join us, there is absolutely no need to have a bed *this* big. As I ponder Oliver's thinking behind the humongous beds, I stretch out my legs on the plush carpet. I lay there for a while, half listening to the rain battering against the windows, half fighting the urge to drift off. It must be at least twenty minutes before I finally drag myself up and make up the other guest bedrooms. Once I am satisfied that the apartment is suitably dressed for our impending guests, I swap my coffee for a glass of water and head for the bathroom.

Perching on the edge of the tub, I watch in tired amazement as the water turns to glistening bubbles before my eyes. I have been so busy this past week that my usual nightly soak has been replaced with a quick run under the shower. It's fair to say that this dip in the bath is way overdue. Far too exhausted to fetch a bottle of wine from the kitchen, I strip down to my birthday suit and climb into the water. The soapy suds provide delicious warmth as I slip my shoulders under the water. Immediately every muscle in my body starts to relax. As much as I love Oliver and Lianna, some alone time is exactly what the doctor ordered.

My wedding band sparkles under the bright bathroom lights as I twirl it around my finger aimlessly. I used to think that being married would feel totally different to just being someone's girlfriend or partner, but to be honest, it really doesn't. Although I must admit that every time I catch a glimpse of my ring, I feel like the luckiest girl in the world. It's hard to believe that after all this time Oliver still makes me go weak at the knees. Before we got married, I heard so many horror stories of the passion being drained from a relationship the second that a ring goes on a man's finger. Luckily, Oliver and I are happier than ever. Feeling a soppy smile play at the corner of my lips, I tell myself to get a grip.

Thinking of my husband, I can't help but wonder what will be waiting for me under the Christmas tree this year. Oliver has always been great at buying gifts. From the exquisite diamond earrings last year, to the beautiful designer handbag that landed on the doorstep for my birthday, somehow he always manages to get it spot on. I wish I could say the same about my own present buying skills. Less than two weeks to go and I *still* haven't got the faintest idea of what to buy him. Maybe I will have to resort to an M&S voucher, because you can never have too many socks, can you?

Telling myself that I will somehow come up the best present ever, I reach for my towel and pull the plug to release the water. Thank God for under floor heating. Without it, it is very possible that I would make it through the entire winter as one very sweaty Betty. Watching the raindrops turn to sleet, I tug on a pair of fluffy pyjamas and dive under the covers. Usually, I miss going to bed alone, but being able to sleep in the starfish position is a treat not to be sniffed at. Flicking off the light, I snuggle down beneath the sheets and let out an almighty yawn. Christmas might be just around the corner, but so are my parents and I don't know which one is going to be more stressful.

A holiday miracle would be me fitting into my clothes AFTER the holidays.

December 13th

'We're going to be late!' I grumble, clutching Oliver's very cold hand as we squeeze our way through the crowd of slow-moving people. 'I *told* you that we should have set off earlier.'

Not bothering to reply, Oliver shakes his head in disagreement and carries on walking through the busy airport. I *hate* being late. Especially as I promised my parents that we would most definitely be on time. With Marc giving us both an early finish we should have been here over an hour ago, but Oliver insisted that we had time to grab a burger before for the rush hour. To cut a long story short, we hit the McDonald's drive-through and then sat in a very cold car for a very long time. Needless to say, I am *not* a happy bunny. What is it with men thinking with their stomachs over their brains?

Finally coming to a stop outside Arrivals, my eyes scan the hordes of people for our parents. To be fair, they shouldn't be too hard to find. Janie and Randy's Texas accents will stand out like a sore thumb amongst the quiet babble of British voices. Standing on my tip toes for a better look, I smile as a trio of excited children throw themselves into the arms of a returning solider. Trying not to shed a tear at their delighted squeals, I entwine my fingers with Oliver's. What is wrong with me lately? The slightest thing sends me on an emotional roller coaster. I even teared up at an Andrex advert yesterday. Just thinking about those adorable puppy dog eyes gives me a lump in my throat. I really need to get a grip.

Running a finger under my eyes in a bid to stop the tears from falling, I spot a couple of Santa hats bobbing along through the sea of people and shake my head as I realise who they belong to.

'Oh, God.' I mumble, taking a deep breath. 'They're here.' Fixing a smile onto my face, I raise a hand in acknowledgement.

Singing Christmas songs loudly and laughing like a pack of teenagers, they are obviously rather inebriated. It looks like they have been taking full advantage of the all inclusive drinks on board the plane. Oliver lets out a groan which quickly escalates to a laugh as he greets his parents with open arms. Turning my attention to my own parents, I pull my dad in for a bear hug and squeeze him tightly.

'Dad!' I stand back to give him a quick

once over. 'You look fantastic!'

He really does. His usual porcelain skin has a lovely golden glow and his familiar tired eyes are bright and sparkling. It looks like this impromptu break away has done Henry Andrews the world of good. 'How was your flight?'

'Ask your mother.' Rolling his eyes, he motions over to my mum.

Happily jingling the bells on her hat, she seems to be having a whale of a time.

As I wait for her to prise herself away from Oliver, I reach up and greet Oliver's dad with a kiss on the cheek. 'Hi, Randy. How are you?'

Squeezing him tightly, I listen intently as he tells me just how excited he is to be spending his first Christmas in the UK. My stomach churns as he reels off a list of very British Christmas traditions that he can't wait for. Oh, dear. Christmas crackers and paper hats I can do, but Yorkshire puddings and traditional English trifle *might* prove a little trickier. Maybe I will fake a fall and make my mum do the cooking instead. No one can be mad at a sous chef on a stretcher, can they?

'Clara!' My mother's voice pierces my thought bubble, bringing me back down to Earth with a bump.

'Mum!' Letting out an excited squeal, my

eyes widen as I take in my mum's appearance.

It might have been only a couple of months since I last saw her, but once again she looks totally different. If the blonde highlights were a shock, then this new look is most certainly going to take a bit of getting used to. With the jet-black bob and hot pink lips, you would be forgiven for thinking that she was auditioning for the lead in Snow White. Just to clarify, I do mean Snow White, *not* the Evil Queen. That role is being saved for Janie.

'You look... incredible.' Running a hand over her sleek new do, I link my arm through hers. 'I'm so glad that you're here.' And Christmas dinner panic aside, I really am pleased to see them.

'Where's my favourite daughter in law?' A husky Texan drawl that is instantly recognisable pipes up from the crowd.

Wearing a sparkly Christmas jumper with two strategically placed mince pies, I ignore the rude slogan and greet her with a smile. To anyone else, a sixty-something woman wearing spiky Louboutins, a lewd jumper and far too much make up would be rather shocking, but as someone who knows her, you have to believe me that this as conservative as it gets.

'Janie!' Spinning around at the sound of

Janie's voice, my lips stretch into a smile as I take in my mother-in-law.

'You're looking a little... fuller figured.' Janie muses, prodding me in the ribs and letting out a ridiculously loud cackle. 'I'm kidding!' She yells, before I have the chance to throw a tantrum.

Not wanting to get into an argument straight away, I punch her playfully in the arm and grit my teeth. It's fair to say that Janie and I have had our ups and downs over the past few years, but I have to admit that I have grown rather fond of her in recent times. When Oliver and I first met, I thought that Janie was going to be the world's worst monster in law. Needless to say, things have improved greatly between us and I would even go as far as to say that she has become a very good friend. A very good friend who is sarcastic, super critical and a bit of a bitch, but still.

'Let's get outta here.' Oliver announces, grabbing hold of his mother's suitcase. 'Who's hungry?'

Randy lets out a whoop as we start to make our way back to the car park. I hope they are all up for beans on toast. I hear the word takeout thrown around and breathe a sigh of relief. Thank God for Dominos.

* * *

Turning up the fire, I grab another bottle of red from the wine rack and proceed to top up everyone's glass. Being the hostess, I decided to stick to orange juice and to be honest, it has been rather fun watching everyone else get merry and loose-lipped whilst keeping a clear head. It's rather entertaining to see other people losing their inhibitions safe in the knowledge that you aren't making a fool of yourself, too.

Placing the now empty bottle onto the coffee table, I curl up on the sofa next to Oliver and stretch out my legs. After a little disagreement over who was having the bigger guest bedroom, tonight has been a huge success. Thankfully, Lianna offered to kip on the sofa which nipped the argument in the bud before it got out of hand. Given that she is officially moving into her new place tomorrow, I don't think that one night on a plush, leather sofa bed will do her any harm.

'I just *love* Christmas.' Janie declares, draining her glass in one swift gulp. 'My favourite holiday.'

'Really?' Oliver raises his eyebrows questioningly. 'I thought Fourth of July was your favourite holiday?'

'Any holiday where it is socially

acceptable to drink before noon is your mother's favourite holiday.' Randy laughs loudly and bangs his hand down on the table.

Janie mumbles something under her breath and reaches for a handful of nachos. Wow! Christmas really must be her favourite holiday. I don't think I have ever seen Janie eat a carb before. In fact, I distinctly remember her saying that she hasn't eaten carbs in years. Catching Randy's face crease with laughter as he locks eyes with Janie, I feel a smile play at the corner of my mouth. The only thing more beautiful than young love is old love. Not that I'm calling Janie old, obviously. I would rather pick a fight with Tony Montana than have Janie find out that I have used her name and the word *old* in the same sentence.

'Anyone want this last slice of pizza?' Lianna asks, licking her lips greedily as she eyes up the remainder of the Meat Feast.

Before anyone has the chance to respond, she picks up the slice and takes a giant-sized bite, stopping only to wipe a dollop of barbecue sauce off her nose. I'm going to miss having Lianna around. Yes, she is a messy, dippy airhead, but I have become quite fond of our girly natters over a morning coffee. I don't think I can say the same for Oliver. Having to fight two girls for the bathroom hasn't gone down very well. On more than one occasion this week he has grabbed his rucksack and announced that he would be having a shower at the gym. I dread to think how he would cope with a houseful of children to contend with. Maybe this is why so many men end up with a man cave. If married life has taught me anything, it's that boys never really grow up. They just get older and have bigger, more expensive toys.

'Are you sure you don't want a drink?' Oliver asks, tucking a stray strand of hair behind my ear.

Shaking my head in response, I lean back and rest my head on his shoulder. No matter how cold it is outside, for some inexplicable reason Oliver is always toasty and warm. I wish I could say the same for myself. It only has to drop below room temperature for my hands and feet to turn into blocks of ice. Lianna jokes that it's because I'm cold-hearted, but my argument is that I was born in the wrong body. I'm totally convinced that I was destined for a remote Caribbean island and to be basking in forty degree heat. With a Pina Colada and a copy of Cosmopolitan, *obviously*.

Oliver runs his fingers down my spine

and I enjoy the feeling of his gentle touch on my skin. If I ever win the Lottery, I am going to pay someone to do this to me all day long. I'd also have a live-in hairdresser to blow dry my wild curls. Glossy, straight hair is a luxury you can only really appreciate if you have a crazy, animal like mane like mine. Feeling my eyelids start to get heavy, I turn onto my side and watch the Christmas tree lights twinkle vibrant shades of red and gold. From my position on the sofa, I can see hundreds of tiny people on the dark streets below, clutching shopping bags and playing around in the freshly fallen snow.

So grateful to be out of the cold, I listen to the laughter that is filling the room and let out a sigh of relief. Everyone is smiling, suitably fed and toasty warm. The fire crackles quietly, providing a lovely background noise to the pretty scene. It's a little early to say, but I have a funny feeling that Christmas at the Morgan's might just be a success after all.

All I want for Christmas is you.
Just kidding.
Get me diamonds.

December 14th

'It's moving day!' Lianna squeals, jumping onto our bed and diving in between Oliver and myself like an overly excited toddler. 'Come on! Wake up!'

Peeling open an extremely tired eye, my brow creases into a frown as Lianna shakes me roughly. 'What time is it?' I ask, my voice hoarse as I try to block out the bright morning light.

'It's moving time!' Her voice is so high pitched it actually hurts my ears just listening to her. 'Come *on*! Today's the day that you're finally going to get rid of me.'

'OK!' I surrender, not wanting to be subjected to her screeching for a moment longer. 'Just give me a few minutes to wake up properly.'

I pull a pillow over my head and stretch out my legs in a bid to breathe some life back into them. Oh, what I wouldn't give for five more minutes of delicious sleep. Rolling off the bed and yanking open the curtains she turns her attention to a sleepy Oliver. 'Rise and shine, Mr Morgan. We're going to need those muscles of yours today.'

Letting out a groan that resembles a bear with a sore head, Oliver pulls the duvet up over his head and rolls over. From the looks of things, I don't think that he will be moving anytime soon. Pushing myself up onto my elbows, I look out of the window and I'm pleasantly surprised to see that it isn't raining. Yes, it's cloudy and looks colder than ever, but at least it is dry for the first time in weeks.

'Come on!' Lianna shouts again, motioning towards the door. 'What have I got to do to get you both up?'

'Bacon.' Oliver growls from beneath the sheets. 'And coffee. Lots of coffee.'

*　*　*

An hour and a half later we arrive at Lianna's new house with our caffeine levels in over drive. Well, when I say we, I mean, Lianna, my mother, Janie and myself. We decided over breakfast that if we had any hope at all of getting this done in one day, we were going to have to split up into two groups. After a little deliberation, we agreed that the boys would collect the furniture from Lianna's mother's house whilst the girls unpack the mountain of clothes that are already here. Any outsider would think that the girls got the easier job, but Li has more clothes than Donna

Karen and Donatella Versace put together.

'Ready?' Lianna asks, turning off the engine. 'I've made a start on the decorating but it still needs some work... just use your imagination.'

Flashing me a shy smile she throws open the door and runs up the garden path, not bothering to wait for the rest of us to catch up. I weigh up the dark grey sky and decide to make a run for it before the heavens open and we end up drenched again. It's fair to say that Janie was less than impressed at being soaked by the good old English weather this morning. My blood ran cold when I heard her terrifying screams, only to discover that the commotion was the result of a few drops of rain.

Turning around in my seat, a grin spreads across my face as I watch Janie weigh up the clouds dubiously. 'Do you want to borrow my hat?' I ask, tearing off my knitted ski hat and passing it between the seats.

'What the hell is that thing?' Taking it with the tip of one of her hot pink acrylics, her revulsion is clear to see. 'I'd rather wear road kill.'

My mum lets out a little giggle and I throw her a stern stare. Snatching back my hat, I tug it on and make a sound that lets them know I am far from impressed. We haven't even stepped foot out of the car and already they are getting on my nerves. I have got a feeling that today is going to be a *very* long day.

As Janie fashions an umbrella out of a couple of old magazines, I brave the cold trudge through the sludge to the front door. Letting myself in, I am pleasantly surprised. The first thing that hits me is the distinctive smell of fresh paint. Lianna was right, she really has been decorating. Wandering along the hall I run my fingers across the beautiful new wallpaper and shake my head in disbelief. She must have done all this on her own. I did wonder what on Earth she was doing sleeping here on her own the past couple of nights.

I pop my head into the living room and actually let out a little gasp. The worn floorboards that the last time I was here were dusty and scratched, are smooth, glossy and frankly, look rather amazing. A single wall has been painted a gorgeous shade of green. A near empty tin of paint on the windowsill informs me that it is *subtle sage*. Nodding my head in approval, I make my way into the kitchen. Wow! It looks like she has been working her magic in here, too. Bright red tiles line the new worktops and splashes of classic navy have been dotted around the room. The dark horse, if I knew that she was this good at interior design I would have had her spruce up the guest bedroom whilst she was at ours.

'What do you think?' Lianna asks as she runs down the stairs excitedly. 'I know I haven't done much yet, but you can get the feel of the look I am going for.'

'I think it's fantastic!' I reply, draping an arm around her shoulder encouragingly. 'Have you done all this yourself?'

She nods in response and leads me to the master bedroom. 'This is my favourite part.'

Throwing open the built in wardrobe, I let out a gasp as she flicks on the light. The entire unit has been knocked through to make a giant walk in closet. Shoe rails line either side and at the far end is a long rail that is just waiting to be dressed in amazing dresses, coats and bags. *Jealous* isn't the word.

'I want one.' I mumble, trying not to feel envious.

'Well, you better put it on your Christmas list, because this one's *all* mine...'

* * *

'Is that the last of it?' Oliver hollers across the garden to Randy who shoots him the thumbs up sign in response. 'Thank God!'

Collapsing onto Lianna's pretty new sofa, he kicks off his shoes and lets out a super-sized yawn. It might have taken us until almost midnight, but between the seven of us, we have *finally* moved everything in. Looking around the now cosy house, I have to admit that we have done pretty well. It's safe to say that we have transformed the blank canvas into a lovely house that Lianna will be proud to call her home.

Although the girls have done a great job with the interior of the house, the biggest thank you of the day has to go to Oliver and Randy. For hours on end, they have ferried furniture from the other side of town. It seems that sofas, televisions and kitchen equipment are a *lot* heavier than they look and carrying them is made even more difficult by the fact that is freezing outside. Technically, I should be crediting my father with the boy's hard work, but his bad back excluded him from any major lifting. Instead, he declared himself *logistics manager* and spent the majority of the day barking orders at the rest of us.

Deciding that our hard work deserves to be rewarded, I make a grab for Lianna's car keys.

'I think this calls for a celebration.' I mumble to Oliver as I tug on my shoes. 'I'll nip to the supermarket and get a bottle of fizz.'

'Do you think that's wise with everything that will be happening tomorrow?' Raising his eyebrows tellingly, he sends me a mental SOS which I decode immediately.

'Oh...' I reply, suddenly remembering about Li's surprise birthday party. 'Maybe you're right.'

It's a running joke amongst our social group about Lianna's ability to drink a bottle of Tequila and wake up fresher than a teenage girl at summer camp, but unfortunately this can't be said for the rest of us. The thought of having to attend a birthday party with a raging hangover makes me feel a little queasy.

'Who wants a scotch?' Janie demands, rather than asks, handing each of us a rather large glass of whiskey.

Not daring to say no, I take the golden liquid dubiously and shoot Oliver a worried look. He knows more than anyone just how hard his mother is to say no to. Looking around the room at just how happy everyone looks, I decide that one small glass couldn't hurt. Lianna's eyes sparkle as she video calls Marc and Gina to show them the result of our hard work. Watching her proudly give them a tour of her new home, I snuggle into Oliver's chest happily. Thank God we managed to get her sorted out. Looking at her now it's hard to believe that just a couple of weeks ago she turned up on our doorstep with nothing but tears in eyes and a battered holdall. It just goes to show that with great friends by your side, you really can get through anything...

I'm dreaming of a white Christmas,
but if the white runs out,
I'll drink the red...

December 15th

'What do you think?' Lianna asks, twirling around to show me her outfit of choice for the evening. 'Don't I look cool?'

Eyeing up the retro Dr Martens and ripped dungarees dubiously, I bite my lip as I try to think of a suitable response. Don't get me wrong, she looks great. Totally rocking this season's geek chic, but I don't even think that she would be allowed inside Snowflake dressed like this. This is the problem with surprise parties. Li thinks that she is having a casual curry at our local Indian restaurant and has dressed for the part perfectly. However, Snowflake is more of a *who* are you wearing rather than *what* are you wearing kind of place, if you get what I mean. Being the fashionista that she is, I know that she would rather die than be seen dead in Snowflake looking like a reject from the Saved by the Bell fan club, but how do I tell her this without giving away the surprise?

'You haven't said anything for about three minutes so I am guessing that you don't approve.' Squinting her eyes at me, she proceeds to kick off the heavy boots.

'No!' I protest. 'I love the Dr Martens...

it's just that... well... why don't you dress up a little more tonight. It is your birthday after all.'

'We're going to *Saffron*.' Li looks at me like I have lost my mind as I try desperately to think of a way to encourage her to change.

Saffron is a little Indian street food eatery in town. The surroundings are nothing to write home about and it is almost always full of hoodie wearing students, but they make the best lamb bhuna in the world. To be fair, the idea of getting glammed-up to go to Saffron is actually laughable. Getting her to change is going to be harder than I thought. Pulling my dressing gown tightly around my ice-cold body, I suddenly have an idea.

'Do you know what would be really fun?' I ask, plastering a ridiculous smile on my face and ignoring her annoyed expression.

'What?' She grumbles, folding her arms and throwing herself down onto my bed.

'I could give you a makeover!' My voice is ridiculously high and over pitched, but I really don't care.

'No!' She fires back stonily. 'Absolutely no chance.'

'Oh, come on! Today is the day that you turned thirty. Let's mark this new chapter in your life with a whole new look.' I'm trying to make this sound as exciting as possible, but I am already aware that I am failing miserably.

As soon as the word *thirty* escapes my lips, I know I have made a big mistake. Up until now, Lianna had been surprisingly upbeat considering her recent meltdown, but the look on her face right now tells me that we have just taken a huge step back.

'Actually, I think I would prefer to stay in tonight.' Li's voice is quiet as she grabs the remote and flicks on the television. 'I'm too tired to go out.'

'No!' I yell, a little too loudly. 'We *have* to go out. Oliver has made reservations.'

'So...' Burying herself under the duvet, she lets out a loud sigh.

I look down at my watch in a mild panic as I realise that I have just one hour to get Lianna out of this sulk and into a decent outfit. Oh, God. I had *one* job. My only responsibility was to get her to the bloody place on time without her knowing. Marc will kill me if I screw this up.

Tugging off the duvet, I slide in beside her and poke her in the ribs gently. 'Li? Turning thirty doesn't have to be a big deal. You're looking at it all wrong.'

Lianna doesn't say anything, but the fact that she doesn't burst into tears at the mention of the big 3-0 is something at least.

'Instead of wallowing over the things that you haven't achieved yet, you should be taking this huge milestone as the chance to start a new chapter in your life. You have a clean slate, a brand new decade to create the life that you always wanted.'

There is slight movement under the covers and I know that I am winning. She pokes her head out of the sheets and curls one corner of her mouth into a half smile.

'Now you're going to get up, put some lipstick on and pull yourself together. OK?'

* * *

'You look incredible.' Oliver mouths, visibly very impressed.

'Doesn't she?' I agree proudly, as Lianna shows off the result off her impromptu make over.

Rocking my backless Versace dress and a pair of my much-loved Louboutins, she looks every inch the superstar that she is. Happy that I am halfway to completing my task, I grab my lipstick and apply a slick of red to my lips.

'Ready?' Oliver asks, as a cab pulls up outside.

'Ready as I'll ever be.' Lianna smiles and

makes for the door, taking extra care not to fall over in the ridiculously high heels.

'Don't you need a jacket?' I hold out a black blazer, but she shakes her head and tosses her hair over her shoulder confidently. 'But you're going to freeze!'

'Clara, I think you will find that I am now old enough to make my own decisions. Even if I know they are totally stupid.'

Tossing my blazer onto the couch, I grab my clutch bag and follow her down the slushy path. 'That's my girl.'

* * *

'This driver has absolutely *no* idea where he is going.' Lianna presses her nose up against the cold glass and attempts to get a proper glimpse of where we are going.

Thankfully, the fact that the night sky is a powerful shade of black makes it difficult for her to see exactly where we are. I lock eyes with Oliver and try to get him to distract her from the window.

'Blackstone Street is closed. He's probably following a diversion.' He scratches his nose and looks down at his feet nervously.

Gosh, he really is a terrible liar. Stifling a giggle, I sit back in my seat and try to send a discreet text message to Marc. Typing without looking at the screen is not as easy as it looks. After three or four failed attempts, I finally click *send* and inform Marc that we are just a couple of minutes away. I cannot wait to see Li's face when she realises what is happening. A frisson of excitement bubbles in the pit of my stomach as I see the iconic Snowflake sign glowing in the distance. Grabbing Olivier's hand, I give it a little squeeze and try not to give the game away.

The taxi comes to a steady stop outside Snowflake and I smile widely as Lianna spins around in her seat looking totally confused.

'Snowflake?' Her brow creases in confusion as she tucks a stray strand of blonde hair behind her ear. 'What are we doing here?'

'We are here for you!' I squeal, clapping my hands together excitedly.

Lianna's jaw drops open as Oliver slips the driver a handful of notes and holds open the door. 'You ready, birthday girl?'

* * *

'Surprise!' The glistening room erupts into raucous noise as Lianna steps into view.

'Arghhh!' Li squeals, jumping up and down and clapping her hands ecstatically. 'Oh... my... God!'

Taking a step back, I laugh happily as Lianna is dragged into the crowd of people, each one wanting to squeeze her tightly and shower her in gifts. A chorus of happy birthdays echo around the room as party poppers explode overhead, covering us in a layer of pink and purple glitter. Scanning my surroundings, I realise that I had forgotten just how cool this place really is. The funky igloo shaped booths have been dressed up with sparkly birthday bunting and a cool white Christmas tree stands proudly in the centre of the room. Hundreds of beautifully wrapped gifts sit underneath the branches, waiting patiently to be ripped open by the birthday girl. A giant number 30 balloon floats around on the dance floor, happily bobbing along to the pumping music. How could turning thirty get any cooler than this?

Lianna tears herself away from the crowd and runs into my arms, her face alight with happiness. 'I can't believe this! Thank you so much!'

'Don't thank me. This was all Marc's idea.' I admit, removing a clump of Lianna's hair from my lip gloss. 'He planned it, he paid for it and he even chose the decorations all by himself.'

'Really?' Her eyes widen in shock as she processes what I have just said.

I have to admit it, I am shocked, too. Although Marc is our boss and our closest male friend, it is rather out of character for him to put so much effort into something like this. Marc's usual acts of kindness don't extend further than a bottle of Rioja and a Meat Feast pizza, so it's understandable that we would find this a little weird. To be honest, with everything else that has been going on lately I haven't really put much thought into it, but now that I have said it out loud it *is* pretty strange.

'Marc!' Li yells above the music, trying to get his attention.

I stand back and watch as Marc and Gina try to squeeze their way through the sea of buzzing people who are chattering loudly. I have to hand it to him, he really has managed to pull this off spectacularly well.

'Happy Birthday!' Gina squeals, throwing her arms in the air and twerking like a deranged monkey. 'Did we surprise you?'

'Are you kidding?' Li exclaims. 'I've never been more surprised in my entire life!'

Laughing as Gina fills Lianna in on just how difficult it was to keep this a secret, I can't help but notice Marc twitching uncomfortably in the background.

'Everything OK?' I ask, sidling up beside him.

'Yeah...' He mumbles, not looking me in the eye.

Not believing him, I weigh up my old friend carefully. His longer than usual locks have started to curl at the ends and his iconic thick rimmed glasses are sliding down his sweaty nose. He looks far from OK.

'What is it?' I press, pulling him around a corner where I can hear him better. 'What's wrong?'

'Nothing.' He attempts a little laugh, but it doesn't quite reach his eyes.

'Come on, Marc! I've known you for long enough to know when you're lying. Spit it out.'

'Honestly, Clara. Everything's fine.'

Squinting my eyes at him suspiciously, I turn around at the sound of my name.

'Clara!' Oliver pops his head into our conversation and holds out his hand. 'Drink?'

Nodding in response, I take his hand and let him lead me across the dance floor. We have only been in here for half an hour and already the music is pumping and the dance floor is alive with gyrating people. I spot Lianna and Gina posing for selfies in front of the Christmas tree and let out a little giggle. I *knew* that she would love this. Raising my hand in acknowledgement, I run over to photobomb their picture. I stick my tongue out and wait for the flash before bursting into a fit of laughter.

'Awwh!' Gina sighs, looking at the photo on her phone. 'I'm going to miss you guys *so* much.'

'Oh, behave. You're only going for two weeks!' Li snatches the phone out of her hand to take a look at the photo.

'Marc hasn't told you?' Gina's brow creases into a frown as her eyes widen. 'He *hasn't* told you, has he?'

'Told us what?' Lianna demands, folding her arms.

'We're going to Australia.' Gina exhales loudly and bites her lip.

'Yeah...' I mumble, trying to work out what has gotten into her.

'No, you don't understand.' Lowering her voice to little more than a whisper, she pulls us in close. 'We're... we're thinking of emigrating.'

'What?' Li and I shout in unison.

Feeling totally flummoxed, I lock eyes with Lianna and try to gather my thoughts. 'Gina?'

'We're emigrating.' She repeats, biting

her lip. 'Well, at least we are seriously thinking about emigrating. I'm sorry. I thought that Marc had told you.'

My heart beats hard in my chest as I try to digest what she has just said. I suddenly feel rather sick. They can't move to Australia! It's the other side of the world for crying out loud. Feeling tears prick at the corners of my eyes, I scan the room for Oliver and catch Marc walking towards us.

'Marc! What the hell is going on?' My voice is hoarse as I try not to show how upset I am. Gina just told us that you are... *emigrating*.' A lump forms in my throat as he takes off his glasses and runs a hand through his hair.

'I was going to tell you both tomorrow.' Putting an arm around Lianna's shoulders, he pulls her over. 'I didn't want to ruin your party.'

'But... but... I don't *care* about the party.' Lianna wails. 'You can't leave! I won't let you.'

Marc lets out a laugh and shakes his head. 'Nothing is set in stone, but it *is* something that we are looking into. We're going to take this next couple of weeks to check out some properties, take a look at the local schools and get a general feel for the place. Don't worry. If we do decide to go, you girls will be the first to know.'

Not feeling any more reassured by his efforts, I look up at him mournfully and offer him a small smile. Talk about a turnaround. Five minutes ago I was happy as can be and now I feel like I have taken a blow to the stomach. Marc has been such a big part of my life for so long, I can't imagine him being on the other side of the world.

'Just think of the free holidays, barbecues on the beach and hot surfer guys. Trust me, if we *do* decide to go, this could be amazing for all of us.'

I notice Lianna's frown ease a little at the mention of surfers and try not to laugh. I guess he is right. Leaving the buzz of the busy city behind for the beach bum lifestyle of down under does sound pretty amazing, even if it pains me to say so.

'Now can we forget about this for tonight, please? In case you have forgotten, today isn't about me, it's about a certain amazing girl who is thirty and fabulous.' Flashing Li a wink, he motions to the bar as the music turns up a notch. 'Come on, let's get a drink.'

Stretching my face into a smile, I rub Lianna's arm encouragingly and follow Marc and Gina to the bar. I can't let them see how gutted I really am, it wouldn't be fair to make this all about me and my own selfish feelings. As Marc said, tonight is about Lianna and I'm going to make sure she has a great birthday if it kills me.

Dear Santa,
Before I try to explain... just how much
do you already know?

December 16th

Stretching out my legs on the soft sheets, the first thing that hits me is how bloody cold it is. The second thing that hits me is that I feel like I have been run over. It takes me a moment to realise that the reason that I feel so dreadful is that last night was Lianna's surprise birthday party. Burying my head into my pillow, I squeeze my eyes tightly shut and desperately try to get back to sleep. A wave of nausea washes over me and I am suddenly wide awake. After Marc's revelation, I only had a couple of drinks last night. News of your best friend leaving the country is kind of a mood killer.

Kicking off the covers onto a snoring Oliver, I clasp my hand to my mouth and make a run for the bathroom. The ice-cold tiles beneath my bare feet do little in making me feel better. With my head down the toilet and my arms wrapped around the basin, it is safe to say that I am feeling rather sorry for myself. Once I am confident that my stomach is finally empty, I strip myself of my pyjamas and dive into the shower.

Enjoying the hot water pummelling into

my back, I swear to myself that I will not be drinking alcohol *ever* again. Sometimes I forget that I am a married woman now. Vomiting into the toilet like an eighteen-year-old girl, who has had one too many alcopops, is *not* how I pictured myself as a wife. Before I met Oliver, I had cooked up images of a cookie baking, twin set wearing Clara with a Waitrose loyalty card. Hilarious, I know.

Grabbing a towel and turning off the shower, I wipe the condensation from the bathroom mirror and stare at my reflection. The remnants of last night's mascara have taken up residency below my eyes and my skin looks positively green. Deciding that from this moment on I will be a changed woman, I shove a toothbrush into my mouth and wander over to the window. Snowflakes fall from the grey sky and dissolve into slush as they hit the concrete below. I've never known a December to have so much snow before. I remember being a child going to bed praying for snow on Christmas Eve and still waking up to the same old clouds and rain.

Placing my toothbrush back into its holder, I pad back into the bedroom and place my ear against the door. No sounds of movement coming from the living room which can only mean that the others are still asleep. My eyes land on the calendar at my bedside and I feel a rush of anxiety run through my body. Only nine days to go until Christmas Day. Nine days to pull off the perfect Christmas for our families. At least Lianna is finally sorted. Now that I don't need to worry about her I can fully concentrate on the task at hand. Facing up to what I have to do makes me more than a little concerned that I am going to royally mess things up.

As I drag on my jeans and a fluffy jumper, my phone vibrates loudly from my bag on the floor. Bending down to retrieve it, I squint my eyes to focus on the screen and tap to open the email.

All customers who have pre-ordered a turkey from our finest selection will be available to collect their order from stores tomorrow.

Laughing at the absurdity of pre-ordering a bird, I shake my head and toss my phone onto the bed. Some people really need to get a life.

'Ow!' Oliver grumbles from beneath the covers as the handset lands on his stomach.

'Sorry!' Retrieving the phone from the bed, I flop down beside him and bring the email up on the screen. 'Can you believe this? People actually *pre-order* poultry!'

'You are kidding?' Pushing himself up onto his elbows, he pushes his hair out of his eyes. 'You *have* ordered us a turkey, right?'

Laughing at his sarcasm, I stretch my arms up above my head and let out a loud yawn. Even though we have been together for so long, I still find it difficult to work out if he is kidding or not.

'Clara?' His voice is suddenly more serious.

'What?'

'You do remember last year? When all the stores in a fifteen-mile radius sold out of turkey?' Throwing back the covers, he reaches for a pair of jeans. 'Jesus Christ, Clara.'

Feeling my cheeks turn a violent shade of red, I look down at my feet and curse myself for being so stupid. Of course, I was meant to pre-order the bloody turkey! Last year we spent no less than five hours running from supermarket to supermarket desperately seeking a bird of some kind. In the end, we resorted to a lamb shank and had to make the most of it.

Not daring to look him in the eye, I stand up and grab the car keys.

'I'll get my coat.'

I sincerely hope that you like this present more than I did when I received it last year...

December 17th

'What the hell is this?' Janie asks, poking her head into the fridge and holding out a bag of chopped kale. 'If you think I have travelled nine hours to be fed rabbit food for Christmas then you've got another thing coming lady!'

Tossing the offending bag back into the fridge, she grabs a bottle of wine and sashays over to the couch where my mother is waiting with an empty glass. Honestly, the two of them are like a pair of teenagers.

'Don't worry, Janie. I *promise* I will serve you up a meal to remember.' Biting my lip, I silently pray that it isn't a meal to remember for all the wrong reasons.

After our impromptu trip to the supermarket yesterday, Oliver and I spent the rest of the day watching re-runs of Nigella's Christmas Kitchen online. Needless to say, we are still none the wiser over what we are going to do. Oliver keeps trying to convince me that we can always order takeout from Saffron and more worryingly, I'm only partly convinced that he is joking. Reminding myself that we are hosting for two hungry men and three difficult to please women, I make a mental note to look into hiring a chef for the day. No matter how hard Oliver tries to talk me round, I'm still having a recurring nightmare of us serving up burnt toast with a side of peanut butter. Telling myself that everything will be OK, I grab a bottle of Evian from the fridge and collapse down next to my mother on the couch.

'Water?' She scoffs, waving the bottle of Sauvignon Blanc around wildly. 'What's wrong with you? Are you sick?'

'I'm just still feeling the after effects of Lianna's birthday.' Screwing my nose up to emphasise my point, I smile to myself as the memories of Friday night's antics come flooding back to me.

After Marc and Gina's Aussie bombshell we all had an amazing night. Especially Li, who spent the majority of the evening on the dance floor with a bottle of Champagne in her hand. That's right, bottle, not glass. As she continually reminded me throughout the night, she is *old enough and ugly enough to make her own decisions.*

Now that I have had the time to think about it, I am actually really happy for Marc. He always said that he would love to live in the sun one day and now that he has a little family of his own, I guess the time is right for him to spread his wings and fly. I would just rather he didn't fly all the way to Australia. With Oliver's entire family living in Texas, I can completely understand the urge Gina must have to be with her parents. On a few occasions, Oliver has raised the subject of us moving to America, but for some reason, I have dug my heels in and insisted that we stay in England. Why? I don't really know. I don't have any siblings that I am close to and my parents are always jetting off around the world on various different holidays. It's not like I have a close family unit or anything.

Feeling a lump form in my throat, I glance over to the photo of Marc, Lianna and I on the windowsill. I've never realised it before, but I guess that my friends have always been my family. They do say that friends are the family that we choose for ourselves, don't they? Blinking back the tears, I pull the throw up to my chin and rest my head on my mum's shoulder. Why am I crying again? I swear this whole Christmas thing is giving me anxiety attacks. I really need to pull myself together.

Pushing myself to my feet, I leave the gruesome twosome in the living room and pad into the kitchen, wincing as the waistband of my jeans digs into my stomach. Talk about piling on the pounds. There's still over a week to go and already I am turning into a porker. At this rate, I might as well don my red onesie and label myself Father Christmas, at least that way I will have an excuse for the pot belly. Suddenly feeling more tired than hungry, I slip into the bedroom and leave the rest of the gang to drink themselves into a happy oblivion. It might only be 8.00pm, but I am absolutely exhausted and knowing that I have a long day at work tomorrow makes it an easy decision for me to swap my tight jeans for one of Oliver's t-shirts and climb under the covers.

From my hiding place beneath the sheets, I hear Janie crank up the music and let out a small smile. Whilst I'm being a party pooper, it's good to know that the others are having a good time. My eyelids become extraordinarily heavy as I draw up a mental list of this coming week's activities. With just over seven days to go, it's safe to say that the countdown is well and truly on.

My favourite part of the holiday season is blaming my long-term weight-gain on the holiday season.

December 18th

Pulling my scarf up over my ears to block out Janie's incessant moaning, I shove my hands into the depths of pockets and carry on trudging through the snow. For the past two hours, Janie, my mother, Lianna and I have been scouring the shops for some last-minute stocking fillers - or in Janie's case *actual* stockings. So far, it is fair to say that this little trip has been quite the success. When Li and I stepped out of work this evening to be greeted by the terrible twosome, I have to admit that I wasn't a very happy Clara. For starters, all day I have been dreaming about climbing into my lovely roll top bath with a very large glass of Rioja and a Jo Malone candle. A dream that went straight out of the window at approximately 5.34pm this afternoon.

'This is the best store *ever!* Janie exclaims, clutching a mountain of carrier bags as she pushes her way outside. 'Ann Summers. We have *got* to get one of these back home.'

'You don't have an Ann Summers?' My mother's voice sounds strangely surprised for someone who until last year wore twin sets and pearls.

Not wanting to listen to my mother and mother-*in-law* talk about their sex shop escapades, I link my arm through Lianna's and march ahead.

'Those two are hysterical!' Lianna laughs as we weave our way through the manic last-minute Christmas shoppers. 'I wish my mother was like that.'

'No, you really don't.' Lianna's mother is one of those straight-talking business types who are super critical 99.9% of the time, although her heart is in the right place. 'Your mum might be a lot of things, but embarrassing isn't one of them.'

'Are you kidding me?' She scoffs. 'Do you not remember last year's Christmas party?'

'Oh...' Having a flashback to twelve months prior, I suddenly remember Li's mother stripping down to her smalls and giving Chris from the I.T department a lap dance.

'Maybe you've got a point.' I concede, stifling a giggle.

Don't get me wrong, Vanessa Edwards is stunningly beautiful with a body that most teenagers would be envious of, but she still gave poor Chris a heart attack and Lianna almost died on the spot.

'Talking about the Christmas party, are you looking forward to Wednesday?' She asks, dodging the snowballs that are being thrown by naughty children across the street.

'Yeah. I still think that it's a disaster waiting to happen though.'

'So do I, but as long as there's free alcohol, I'm there!'

'Whoa! Hold your horses!' Janie's voice pierces my eardrums as she comes running up behind us. 'Did you just say *free* alcohol?'

* * *

Bursting through the apartment door, I drop my carrier bags and make a run for the fire. After a long day at work, five hours of intense shopping is the equivalent of a triathlon. OK, that might be a little dramatic, but I am honestly wiped out. Thankfully, my lovely husband called as we made our way home and offered to drive out for pizza. Smiling as the smell of freshly baked dough fills my nostrils, I kick off my heavy boots and prop myself up at the kitchen island.

'I knew I married you for a reason.' I nuzzle my face into his warm chest as he grabs a plate and dishes me up a slice. 'How was your day?'

'Busy.' He replies, taking a huge bite of

pizza. 'Luckily, your dad introduced mine to the pub on the corner of Wilson Street so, I have had the entire evening to kick back and relax.'

Feeling a little annoyed that I could have been curled up with a warm Oliver instead of traipsing around the shops when it is below freezing outside, I tuck into my pizza. With having both of our parents here, it has been rather difficult to find time to be alone with each other. Not for anything like that, *obviously*. I mean, we're not animals or anything, but still, it would be nice to have a cuddle on the sofa without worrying about being disturbed by an angry American searching for alcohol.

'I miss you.' Planting a kiss on his nose, I wrap my arms around his neck and rest my head on his shoulder.

'What?' He laughs. 'I'm right here.'

'I know, but I miss it being just the two of us.'

'Well, it is just the two of us.' Planting a hand on my swollen stomach, his eyes glint with excitement. 'Isn't it?'

'Oi!' Almost choking on my pizza, I slap his hand away and suck in my protruding belly. 'In case you didn't know, it's *Christmas* and that means that you are allowed to gain a few pounds!'

Laughing loudly, he ruffles my hair and

takes a gulp of beer. I let out a sound that resembles a disgruntled chipmunk and shoot him a frown. 'When you married me, you promised for better or for worse.' Holding my pizza up to emphasise my point, I carry on talking. 'This is my worse.'

'I'm kidding. Eat your pizza.'

Suddenly not feeling hungry any more, I push the greasy slice around my plate miserably.

'Oh, come on.' Taking my hands in his, he nuzzles his nose against my face. His huge blue eyes stare deep into mine. 'I loved you yesterday, I love you still. Always have, always will.'

And just like that, I fall in love with him all over again.

How do we know that Santa is a man?
Because absolutely
no woman would wear the same outfit
year after year.

December 19th

'Would you like to sit on Santa's knee and tell me what you would like for Christmas?' The Asian Santa Clause asks Lianna mischievously as we take our seats in Saffron.

'You mean... you didn't get my email?' Li holds her hand to her forehead in mock panic and rolls her eyes. 'That guy is a creep.'

'I know and believe it or not, he is even creepier without the costume.' Recognising Santa as Ahmed, our overly friendly delivery driver, I offer him a thin smile and pull out a chair.

With the massive over indulgence lately of chocolate, mince pies and anything roasted, we thought it would be a good idea to take everyone out for Indian food for a change. Now, you are probably thinking that this would be a nice occasion, but Janie turned up her nose at the very first mention of curry. Apparently, spicy food plays havoc with her delicate stomach and the turmeric sets off her asthma. Dramatic just doesn't cover it. Of course, none of us took any notice, we all know the real reason she didn't want to come is that there is a slight possibility she will go over her five hundred calorie a day diet plan. Personally, I find it hilarious that someone who consumes their weight in alcohol before noon could be that bothered about what she eats.

'Could I get you any drinks while you look over the menu?' The friendly waiter asks, passing around a glossy black menu.

'Scotch.' Janie roars. 'Straight up.'

Blimey, she really must be annoyed. On a normal day, Janie's tipple of choice is a scotch on the rocks. In this case, the absence of the ice is noticeable. Perhaps she is trying to give herself a few more calories to play with. Although I wouldn't like to be the one to tell her that ice is calorie free.

'I'm starving.' Oliver declares, licking his lips as he reads through the menu. 'We *are* getting starters, right?'

The entire tables nods in response and places their orders with the waiter. Deciding to go all out, I order a starter, main and a selection of sides before turning to Janie.

'You gotta be kidding me.' Janie mutters under her breath before begrudgingly reeling off her order.

The waiter nods and rushes off clutching his notepad. I *love* spicy food. Especially when it's freezing cold outside and you can feel the chillies warming you up from the inside out. Come to think of it, it has become somewhat of a December tradition for our group to meet up at Saffron more often than what is deemed healthy. I feel a sudden sadness in my stomach as I realise that our friendly gatherings may soon be a distant memory. Glancing over at Lianna, I notice that she also looks a little preoccupied. Perhaps she is thinking the same thing.

'Are you all right?' I lean in closer and notice that she is tapping away on her phone. 'Who are you texting? Is it a boy?'

'Oh, it's... err... nothing! No one.' Plastering a fake smile on her face, she drops her phone into her bag and changes the subject. 'Doesn't it look cool in here?'

Too hungry to get to the bottom of her shifty behaviour, I look around the room and nod in agreement. For a tiny, obscure restaurant, they really do go all out for Christmas. Giant baubles hang from the ceiling and artificial snow has been sprayed on all the windows. Tacky? Maybe. But I for one love it.

'So, did you girls get your shopping sorted yesterday?' Randy's asks, resting his elbows on the table. 'My guess is that we had a pint for every item you bought.

Ain't that right, Henry?'

My dad lets out a half laugh, half cough sound and shakes his head. 'If you believe that, then you haven't seen Rosemary shop.'

'Oh, is that so?' Mum raises her eyebrows and chooses to ignore the shopping remark. 'Remember what Doctor Sidebotham said. *No more than three units per week.*'

I'm about to chip in with the fact that my mum and Janie had drank more than that before they left the house tonight when the waiter returns with our food. The delicious smell of spices and herbs hits my nose as a plate of yummy looking nibbles is placed down in front of me. Not waiting for everyone else, I pick up my fork and dive in greedily. This might seem rude, but I at least want a few bites before Janie starts moaning about the food. The entire table falls into silence as we tuck into our meal. It always makes me laugh how even the loudest of people can be silenced the second they are presented with food.

'Jesus Christ!' Janie's voice thunders across the table.

'What's wrong?' I knew it wouldn't be long before she started.

'This is delicious!' She swoons, licking her lips between bites.

Almost choking on my onion bhaji, I put down my fork and reach for a napkin. 'Really?'

'Finally!' Randy hollers. 'Something you like that isn't cold and green.'

Oliver laughs and jabs her plate with his fork. 'What did you order?'

Janie grabs a menu from an adjacent table and points animatedly at the dish. Squinting my eyes for a better look, I peer over her shoulder.

'Special Spinach Puri. I don't think I have had that one before.' Taking the menu from her, I look down at the ingredients and feel my stomach flip.

Spinach and mushrooms cooked in our special mix of spices and finely chopped garlic.
Served with our famous keema rice.

Keema? Oh, God! I may not be an expert in Indian food, but I am almost positive that *keema* is a type of minced meat. I lock eyes with Oliver as he takes a bite of Janie's food to see what all the fuss is about. Watching the dawning realisation on his face as he swallows, I bite my lip hard. I don't even need to look at him to know that he isn't going to say anything. Not knowing whether to laugh or cry, I turn back to my own food and stay silent. If experience has taught me anything, it's that sometimes saying nothing is the only option. After all, it wouldn't be the first time that Janie has shot the messenger.

*Anyone who doesn't know what to get
me for Christmas obviously
doesn't know
where to buy wine...*

December 20th

   The giant pile of papers on my desk seems higher now than it did this morning. Despite my ongoing efforts, I haven't made more than a pathetic dent in the mammoth task that is sorting out Marc's mail. To be fair, between typing out email responses and filing away contracts, I have spent a lot of my time procrastinating. Not about anything in particular, it's just that for some reason, I find watching the tiny snowflakes that are falling past the window strangely mesmerising.
   With the majority of the office off work until the New Year, it is only myself, Marc, Lianna, Rebecca and a few of the interns that are here. Well, until 7.30pm this evening that is, as tonight is our office Christmas party. Usually, I look forward to our annual get-togethers. Free booze and a free meal, who wouldn't? However, this year I would rather curl up with Oliver and a cheesy chick flick. Not that Oliver watches chick flicks and the odd time he does, he pops on his headphones and plays video games on his phone. Boys will be boys, I suppose.
   Letting out a tired yawn, I allow myself a

long stretch before flicking off my computer screen. Earlier in the week, I foolishly promised Marc that I would help with the pre-party preparations. At the time I was under the influence of extreme tiredness and hunger so I don't think it would stand up in court, but never one to break a promise I decide to stick to my word. Kicking my chair under my desk, I grab my handbag and wander across the office in search of Lianna. Thankfully, even though I am feeling more Scrooge than Santa today, Li is full of festive frolics.

'Are you ready to deck the halls with boughs of holly?' She trills, throwing a bag of tinsel in my direction.

Watching her hammer a piece of mistletoe to the doorway, I have to admit that her Christmas spirit is a little bit contagious. Until now, the only Christmas spirit that I have been having comes in the form of a sneaky shot of brandy in my morning coffee.

'Don't you think that we should move some of the expensive equipment before we start to decorate the place?' I ask, looking around the room dubiously.

'Expensive?' Li screws up her nose and blows a piece of hair out of her face. 'Like what?'

'Like the computers? The copy machine?

The printers?'

She pauses for a second before shaking her head. 'No, I think it will be fine...'

* * *

'Rebecca!' My scream is so loud it can be heard above the pounding music. 'Be careful!'

Laughing hysterically and totally oblivious to the fact that she has just spilt a glass of red wine over Marc's new computer, Rebecca stumbles over to the makeshift dance floor like Bambi on ice. I *knew* this would happen! I just knew it! In an attempt to save the luxury laptop, I whip off my cardigan and frantically try to soak up the spillage. This isn't the only drunken disaster we have had over the course of this evening. Ever the clumsy drunk, Oliver tripped over a cable wire and crashed into the photocopier, George from HR dropped his egg mayonnaise sandwich on the floor which was inevitably trodden into the carpet and that all happened *before* one of the interns puked into the bin. Yes, it is safe to say that it is definitely not wise to hold office parties *in* the actual office.

'Just leave it.' Li waves around her glass wildly and collapses into Marc's plush leather chair. 'No point crying over spilt wine!'

Listening to her cackle like it is the funniest thing that anyone has ever said, I bite my lip in an attempt to stop myself from laughing. Lianna is my favourite drunk person to be around. Her larger than life laugh is comical at the best of times, but when she has had a drink it is frankly hilarious. Deciding to stop playing the part of mother-hen, I kick off my stilettos and drop down into a chair opposite her.

'So, have you made any New Year's resolutions yet?' Lianna slurs, taking a slug of Pino Grigio.

'Not yet.' I answer honestly. 'I haven't really thought about it much, to be honest.'

'Aren't you going to ask me if *I* have made any?' She stretches out her legs on the table and narrowly misses knocking over Marc's very expensive desk lamp.

'OK...' I reply, slightly bemused at her drunken state. 'Have *you* made any?'

'Well, now that you ask... I have.' Waving around her glass to emphasise her point, she rests her elbows on the table. 'I'm going to quit my job.'

'What?' My brow creases into a frown as I try to work if she is joking. 'What the hell are you talking about?'

'I... am... going... to... quit.... my... job.'

She repeats slowly, as if talking to a naughty three-year-old.

'But... why?' Suddenly worried that she is actually serious, I get up and shut the door.

'Why? Hmm, maybe because I have worked here for almost ten years? Maybe because now that I am *thirty* I need to find an actual career? Or maybe because I applied for a job at an Interior Design firm and actually *got it!*' Her voice goes so incredibly high as she screeches those last words that I can barely make out what she is saying.

'No way!' I slam my hands down on the table as she stamps her feet in excitement. 'Where?'

'At East! I was huddled in a sleeping bag feeling all sorry for myself when I filled in the application, but they called the very next day. I only found out last night in Saffron that I had got the job.' Her mouth stretches into a smile as she speaks. 'You're the first person that I have told.'

'Li! This is fantastic news!' I knew that she was hiding something in Saffron!

'Really?' She reaches across the desk and takes my hand in hers. 'I was a little worried how you would react.'

'Why?'

'Because it means that we wouldn't see

each other every day anymore. It means no more lunches in The Bistro, no more Starbucks in the morning, no more after work drinks...' Lianna's bottom lip wobbles slightly and I can see that she is trying to hold it together.

'We could still have after work drinks.' A lump forms in my throat as I realise just how much I would miss my best friend not being here every day.

Before I have the chance to tear up, Rebecca throws open the office door and allows the thumping music to drift in. 'It's time for Secret Santa! Come on!'

Locking eyes with Lianna, I take a deep breath and nod in response as I push myself to my feet. Now is not the time to be getting emotional. As we are dragged onto the dance floor by an inebriated Rebecca, I give Lianna's hand a little squeeze.

In the space of one week, I have discovered that my two best friends are leaving me. Well, unlike Marc, Lianna is just going across town, not to the other side of the world, but it hurts just the same. Deep down, I know that I should be happy for them. After all, my mother once told me that when all is said and done, we only regret the chances we didn't take. I guess now it's my turn to roll the dice and take a chance on my own future, because you never know just how perfect some things can turn out...

When what to my wondering eyes
should appear,
but an extra ten pounds on my thighs,
hips and rear.

December 21ˢᵗ

Thursday morning, I find myself alone in the apartment. Luckily, I booked today and Friday off months ago so I don't need to worry about work until after the New Year. Unfortunately, the same can't be said for Oliver and Lianna who are currently battling the rush hour traffic in sub-zero temperatures. Feeling rather smug at not being caught in the rat race, I turn up the fire and curl up on the couch with a steaming mug of coffee.

With my parents and the in-laws on a trip to Madame Tussauds, I decided to dedicate today to planning our Christmas meal. After weeks of worrying, I am finally going to be proactive about the problem and tackle it head on. Well, if tackling it head on is taking an online cooking course. It was late last night that Lianna emailed me a link to *The Idiot's Guide to Christmas Cooking.* At first, I laughed it off as a joke, but when I noticed that they promised to turn any cookery clutz into a domesticated goddess in just two hours, I decided to buy into one of their online classes. You see, Li might think she is being funny by making a mockery of my limited skills in the kitchen, but I will have the last laugh when she turns up on Christmas Day to a festive feast to make Heston envious.

Sipping my coffee slowly, I glance over at our huge marble dining table and envisage it dressed for the occasion. I can just see it now, turkey with all the trimmings and enough alcohol to sink the Titanic. Although the food might not be up to much, I am one hundred percent confident in my hosting skills. I *was* born and raised by Rosemary Andrews after all and with Lianna's new found love for interior design, I have no doubt that the apartment will be transformed into a wicked winter wonderland. Thinking of Lianna makes my stomach do a little flip. After her drunken babble last night about quitting her job, we didn't get a chance to talk about it again. Between keeping Rebecca away from the drinks table and trying to get red wine stains out of the carpet, I didn't have more than two minutes to myself. Hopefully, she will have a change of heart now that she doesn't have a gallon of wine rolling around inside her.

Draining the contents of my mug, I flick off the television and make my way into the kitchen. My online class is due to start at 10.00am which gives me just under fifteen minutes to get the essentials together. Upon making my payment for the class, I received an email listing all of the supplies that I would need to get the best results. Armed with a blender, various yummy looking ingredients, a few sharp knives and more baking trays than I know what to do with, I tie an apron around my waist and tap my fingers on the worktop impatiently.

Feeling rather smug that I am actually early, I grab my phone and take a few selfies to upload to Instagram. Me wearing an apron and a hair net is definitely something that is in the public interest, or at least Oliver's, who I very much doubt has ever seen me in the kitchen let alone an apron. Pictures uploaded, I dash to the bedroom and get my glasses from the bedside table. Now, I must clarify, I don't technically need glasses for using the computer, but I am secretly hoping that they will make me look a little more intelligent to the other pupils. Not that I should have much competition, I can't imagine that anyone who takes a class entitled *The Idiot's Guide to Christmas Cooking* will be the brightest bulb in the pack.

As I am fiddling with my hair net, the webcam on my laptop springs to life and I am presented with an immaculate mature lady with a perfect blonde bob and distinctly American megawatt smile to match her glossy red pout.

'Hello!' I mumble, waving around a spatula. 'I'm Clara and I am very much looking forward to learning how to cook with you.'

It's only when I stop talking that I realise the beautiful blonde lady can't hear me. It seems that I am to follow the instructions on the screen and call the number below if I have any problems. Humph. Not exactly a *class*, is it? More of a glorified YouTube clip. Feeling a little stung that I have parted with £50 for nothing more than a tutorial, I tear off a chunk of bread and shovel it into my mouth.

Trying to keep a positive mental attitude, I turn up the volume and try to focus on the task at hand. Well, it might not be a one on one with Gordon Ramsay, but it is all that I've got to work with. I listen intently as the blonde lady, who I now know as Pearl E White, talks me through the perfect festive cheesecake. Apparently, the first rule of cooking is that when dealing with more than one course, you start with the dessert first and work your way back. Explains a lot. That must be where I have been going wrong all these years, making my baked potato before diving into the Nutella jar.

Taking the rolling pin that hasn't been used since it was purchased two years ago, I start to bash the digestive biscuits within an inch of their life. Wow! This is actually really fun! See, I knew that I would be good at this if I just put my mind to it. I reach for the blender as instructed and toss the now broken biscuits into the container, followed by the sugar and a ridiculous lump of butter. Now all I need to do is blend the mixture until I get a smooth consistency. Sounds easy enough. This cooking game is a piece of cake, ironically.

Full of confidence, I jab at the *ON* button and wait for the machine to spring into action. When nothing happens, I flip the switch back and forth impatiently. Come on! What is wrong with the damn thing? As I try desperately to get the blender to work, Pearl carries on with her class regardless. Starting to panic that she has now moved on to caramelising the berries, I give the blender a hard whack on the side. For a split second, it begins to whirr before fizzling out into silence. Grabbing the rolling pin in frustration, I repeatedly hit the blender until my arm starts to throb.

Suddenly it kicks into action, only my

heavy bashing has knocked the lid clean off, resulting in sticky, butter soaked crumbs flying all over the kitchen. Letting out an alarmed squeal, I duck under the table to shield myself from the debris. Pieces of biscuit whiz past my eyes like a scene out of a cartoon. And to think this started so well. Tearing off my hairnet, I dig my mobile out of the pocket of my apron and hit speed dial before letting out an exasperated sigh.

'Hi, Ahmed. Yes, it's Clara. Can I place an order for delivery...'

Santa saw your Facebook page.
You're getting a bible
and some suitable clothing for
Christmas.

December 22nd

    Pushing open the door to Suave, I breathe a sigh of relief as the warmth of the building washes over me. Thank God for central heating. When Marc talked Oliver and I into giving him a lift to the airport, I didn't take into account that the six of us plus four enormous suitcases wouldn't fit into Oliver's luxury sports car. Hence why on this very cold afternoon, I found myself collecting the keys to Gina's seven-seater people carrier. No matter how many times Oliver says it, driving one of these is certainly *not* the same as my cute little Hyundai. My arms are throbbing. I feel like I have been steering a bloody tonka-tank around the streets of London.

    With today being the last working day before Christmas, the office is eerily quiet. The usually buzzing reception desk sits in empty silence, the only sign of life coming from the fibre-optic tree in the corner. Checking my watch, I realise that I am early and head off in search of Lianna. As I run up the stairs, I suddenly regret packing on six layers before leaving the house. Making a pathetic attempt to unbutton my parka coat with mitten-clad fingers, I spot

Lianna's familiar blonde locks disappearing into the toilets. Totally out of puff, I tear my bobble hat off my sweaty head and follow her inside.

'Hi.' I whimper, trying to get my breath back. 'How are you?'

'I'm good... I think.' Biting her lip anxiously, she stares at her reflection in the mirror.

Stumbling over to her in my hefty UGG boots, I notice that she is clutching a handwritten letter in her right hand. 'What's that?'

'It's my resignation letter.' She hands it over to me and hops up onto the sink unit. 'I was going to hand it over to Marc before he leaves.'

'Oh.' My heart drops in my chest as I take in the words on the sheet.

For what seems like forever, neither of us says anything. Finally, Li breaks the silence. 'Do you think that I am making a mistake? I mean, it's not as much money and it's all the way across town and apart from doing up the house, I haven't got *any* experience in this what so ever...'

'Lianna...' Interrupting her mid flow, I fiddle with my mittens as I speak. 'If you didn't want the job, then you wouldn't have applied for it and if they didn't think that could do it, they wouldn't have hired you.'

Handing her back the letter, I offer her a thin smile. 'You know what you have to do...'

* * *

'Do you have your passports?' Bouncing MJ on my hip, I watch as Gina does a final run through of all the essentials.

'Passports, boarding passes, insurance documents, money...' Rifling through her hand luggage, Gina flashes me the thumbs up sign. 'I think we're good to go.'

Reluctantly handing over baby MJ, who is securely wrapped up in a zebra print snowsuit, I link my arm through Oliver's to warm myself up. Realising that we had a spare seat in the car, Li decided that she would join us in waving them off. Granted they are only going for a couple of weeks right now, but after the many tears that were shed as she handed in her resignation, she wanted to come along for the ride.

'You *promise* that you are coming back?' Holding on to Marc's arm for dear life, Lianna stares at him intently. 'Because I *will* come over there and find you, you know I will.'

Marc laughs and tosses Madison up in the air. 'Relax! The return tickets are right there in Gina's bag.'

Not one for emotional goodbyes, he wraps an arm around Li's neck and ruffles her hair before taking hold of the suitcase trolley. Knowing that the time has come to wave them off, I chew the inside of my cheek and try to hold it together. Yes, I know that they will be back in just a few short weeks, but the fact that we could very soon be saying goodbye for good makes me want to lose it.

As Lianna hugs Marc and Gina tightly, I scoop up Madison and plant a cold kiss on her cute button nose. 'Are you excited to go on the plane, Madison?'

Not bothering to reply, she wraps her chubby little arms around my neck and rubs her tired eyes. Breathing in her gorgeous baby smell makes my biological clock tick loudly. How can you love something so much that poops all day, screams all night and wipes boogers on your coat? Not wanting to hand her over, I wait until the very last second before sitting Madison on Marc's shoulders.

After wishing them all a safe journey, I sandwich myself between Oliver and Lianna, not wanting to shed a tear until they have disappeared out of sight. We watch in silence as they check in their luggage and make their way across the terminal. With Madison still on his shoulders, Marc stops at the foot of the escalator and turns around. Waving happily, Gina holds MJ on her hip and wraps her free arm around Marc's waist before embarking on the first step. As the escalator elevates them into the distance, I feel a single tear slip down my cheek.

Sensing my sadness, Oliver squeezes my shoulder gently and I try to pull myself together. With all the emotion of today, it's easy to forget that goodbyes don't necessarily mean forever and they most certainly aren't the end. For in this case goodbye just means I will miss you, until we meet again...

Christmas is a time when you get homesick,
even when you're already home...

December 23rd

After all the December hype, it is now just forty-eight hours until the big day and I am feeling positively dreadful. I have never been good at goodbyes, but waking up at the crack of dawn and vomiting is extreme even for me. Very aware that it is coming up to *that* time of the month, I put my severe emotional reaction down to a bad case of PMT. Change has always been something that I have struggled with. Even changing my usual perfume brought me out in hives and that's not solely due to the fact that I bought a cheap copy of the real thing.

Tucking a stray strand of hair behind my ear, I stretch my face into a smile and try to show some enthusiasm as Janie shows off the results of her last-minute shopping trip. Feeling a little delicate, I decided to stay behind with Oliver whilst the two sets of parents braved the shops. As I have failed to open the windows of my advent calendar since December 4th, my lovely hubby and I had a lot of fun devouring the entire lot before we even rolled out of bed. If you can't have chocolate for breakfast at Christmas, when can you?

'That's... lovely, Janie.' I lie, hoping that

I sound convincing. 'Who is that one for?'

Eyeing up the novelty apron dubiously, I dread to think which lucky devil will be presented with this monstrosity on Christmas morning.

'This one's for Randy.' She declares proudly. 'Won't he just love it?'

'Randy?' Not being able to control the laughter that is growing in my stomach, I shake my head incredulously.

'What's wrong?' Janie cackles.

She holds up the apron against her body which makes me laugh even harder. The frankly hilarious apron depicts a rather hunky man with just a Santa hat covering his modesty. The thought of Randy wearing that thing is genuinely hysterical. My mother-in-law and I have had some trying times over the past few years, but I can honestly say that I am going to miss her when she leaves. Having Janie around means that the apartment is always full of life. Sometimes that life is in the form of a drunken rant about the Post Office, but still, it's nice to have some background noise in our normally placid home.

Scuttling back into the spare room with her shopping, she grabs a roll of wrapping paper and slams the door behind her. I must remember to do my own gift wrapping tomorrow. For weeks, I have I put it off and stashed my gifts under the bed, hoping against hope that Oliver doesn't go under there for anything. Not that it would really matter, apart from a cute card there isn't anything else for him. From golf clubs to cuff links, I have racked my brains on a daily basis for the perfect gift, but even now with just one day to go, I still haven't come up with anything. Well, that's not exactly true. My current plan is to dash out tomorrow and hope and pray that the perfect gift just jumps into my basket. Not really a plan, I know.

'I got you something today.' Sitting down beside me, my mother hands me a glossy carrier bag.

'But Christmas isn't until Monday?' Intrigued, I take the bag and cross my legs.

'This isn't for Christmas.' Mum's eyes glint as she pushes the bag towards me. 'Open it.'

Shooting her a suspicious look, I put my hand inside the bag and pull out a beautiful ornate fairy. 'Awwh! It's gorgeous.'

'Isn't it?' She takes the fairy carefully and smooths down her golden hair. 'It's a Christmas tree topper. Don't you recognise it?'

'Should I?' I scrunch up my nose and turn it over in my hands.

Studying the fairy carefully, I rack my brains and try to think where I have seen one like this before. The blonde ballerina bun frames her dainty pixie features perfectly and the full white dress glistens with sparkly snowflakes. Come to think of it, this *does* look strangely familiar.

'Anything?' She presses. 'OK, wait there.' Jumping to her feet, she strolls across the living room and grabs her handbag. Retrieving her purse, she pulls out an old photograph. 'Here.'

Squinting my eyes for a better look, I hold the picture towards the light. It's a photo of me and my dad by a Christmas tree. This must be at *least* twenty-five years old. I turn it over and the date on the back confirms my suspicions. The corners are bent and the colour has almost totally faded. Snowflakes are falling past the window in the background as my dad holds me up high to place a topper on the tree. A stunning blonde fairy topper which is almost identical to the one she has just given me.

'That fairy in the photo belonged to your great grandmother. Obviously, this isn't the same one as that one was sadly damaged in a house move many years ago, but when I saw it in Harrods today I just *had* to have it.' Her voice becomes a little squeaky and she tries a mock cough to cover it. 'My mother passed one down to me and now I would like you to have this one.'

'Awwh!' Feeling completely overwhelmed, I throw my arms around my mother's neck. 'Thank you so much. I love it. I really, really love it.'

'I thought you might and now when you have your own children, you can pass it down to them...'

'Mum!' My cheeks flush pink as I look over my shoulder to make sure that Oliver didn't hear her.

'I'm just saying!' She raises her hands in protest and flashes me a wink. 'No pressure.'

Rolling my eyes, I stand on my tip toes and slot the fairy onto the very tip of the tree. It really is beautiful. I flick on the fairy lights and shoot her the thumbs up sign.

'Merry Christmas, darling.'

'Merry Christmas, Mum.'

Love is what's in the room with you at Christmas, if you stop opening the presents and just listen....

December 24th

Clutching my car keys for dear life, I squeeze my way through the crowd and dive into the safety of my car. Well, I would like to say that risking my life and my mental well-being by hitting the shops on Christmas Eve was worth it, but sadly it wasn't. Scrunching up my receipt for a D&G gift set, I toss the aftershave onto the back seat and start up the engine. After an entire month of searching, my lovely husband is going to wake up to a rather unexciting bottle of aftershave tomorrow morning. Not that there is anything wrong with giving aftershave, it's just that I really wanted to get him something extra special for our first Christmas together as man and wife. Telling myself that it is too late to do anything about his lame gift now, I put the car into gear and pull out of the car park.

If I thought I had won by dodging yesterday's shopping trip I was sorely mistaken. Despite being at the shops just thirty minutes after they opened, the hysteria was already in full force. Queues snaked around the building as shelves were wiped clear by frenzied shoppers, each one desperate to snatch up the last of the

Christmas gifts. I must have spent a good two hours making my way around the shops before realising that it was a choice between a beauty gift set or a partially damaged Furby. Looking at the stereotypical gift set, I think I might have been better to go with the Furby.

As I crawl through the heavy traffic, I feel that classic rush of excitement in my stomach. No matter how old you get, Christmas Eve is always a bit magical. A friend once told me that there's nothing sadder in this world than to awake on Christmas morning and not be a child. When I think back to my first memories of Christmas, I realise that he couldn't have been more right. I can still remember being tucked in bed by my parents after leaving carrots and cookies on the stairs for Santa and his trusty reindeer. That precious rush of anticipation as you run down the stairs as fast your little legs will carry you, desperate to see if Santa has paid you a visit really is priceless.

A smile plays at the corner of my mouth as I get a warm fuzzy feeling inside at recalling such precious memories. Pulling onto the motorway, I suddenly remember our plans for the evening. With it being the night before Christmas, Oliver thought it would be a good idea to test his new surround sound with some classic chrimbo movies and cinema style treats. Granted this might not be the most exciting thing that we could be doing tonight, but a quiet festive evening with my favourite people sounds nothing short of perfection to me...

*   *   *

Tying a silver ribbon around the final gift, I place all six presents under the Christmas tree and stand back to look at my handy work. The gold, embossed wrapping paper shimmers like disco balls under the twinkly lights, just screaming to be opened. Still feeling a little bummed out about Oliver's bog standard gift, I add an extra piece of ribbon to the box and hope he will be distracted from the lame present by my impressive gift wrapping skills.

Following the sound of laughter that is drifting out of the kitchen, I check my watch and I'm surprised to see that it is nearly 7.30pm. Lianna will be here shortly. With her joining us for dinner tomorrow, it made sense for her to come and stay tonight. After all, no one wants to wake up alone on Christmas Day, do they? The delicious smell of popcorn floods my nostrils as I prop myself up at the kitchen table. Bless Oliver. He really has gone all out with his cinema theme. Bowls of popcorn line the worktop, sweet, salted, buttered... you name it, Oliver has bought it. Taking a handful of salted, I munch away as the rest of the group chatters merrily.

It's hard to believe that the seven of us will be sat around this very table in less than twenty-four little hours. The presents have been purchased, the turkey has been prepared (sort of) and the wine is already flowing freely. Christmas has most definitely arrived. Watching Oliver and his dad playing with his new cinema system, I can't help but smile. Boys and their toys. As I am wondering what exactly is so special about a dual unit subwoofer when the intercom buzzes loudly.

'I'll get it.' I yell above the chatter, already knowing that no one is listening. 'Hello?'

'Clara?' Lianna's voice blasts out of the speaker. 'Can you hear the carollers? You all need to come down here. It's pretty incredible...'

* * *

'Jesus Christ! It's freezing out here!' Janie grumbles, rubbing her hands together for warmth. 'This better be good or you won't be getting *anything* tomorrow young lady!'

Stifling a laugh, I zip up my coat as we ride down in the lift. Getting everyone to put down their drinks and head out into the cold night was not easy, but if what I could hear over the intercom is anything to go by, they are going to be glad that they did. The lift doors spring open and we pile out into the lobby as the faint sound of singing seeps into the building. Pushing open the door to the street, I am shocked to see how heavy it is snowing. Thick flakes fall from the sky, covering the entire scene in a soft white blanket. I link arms with Oliver and follow the noise around the corner where I find Lianna.

Wow! She was right, this *is* incredible. Twenty to thirty carollers are huddled around a street light, each one clutching a tea light in a lantern. Wearing Santa hats and Christmas jumpers they really do look magical against the black backdrop of the sky and their voices are almost haunting. A crowd has begun to gather around them as they sing, with passers-by stopping to throw coins into their charity collection. The music gets louder as more people start to join in.

Looking around at my family and best friend, I am touched to see that each one of them is singing along. Despite my best efforts, tears prick at the corners of my eyes. This is what Christmas is about. This right here. It's about love and family. I suddenly realise that it doesn't matter what is waiting for us under the tree, what's really important is who is stood around it...

*It's Christmas in the heart
that puts Christmas
in the air.*

December 25th

Not again. Today of all days. For the third time this week, I throw back the covers and make a dash for the bathroom. Positioning myself over the toilet, I make a poor attempt at holding my hair out of my face. This is getting ridiculous. There is absolutely *no* reason for me to be doing this now. I have made my peace with the possibility of Marc leaving, I haven't had more than a mere sip of alcohol and I'm pretty darn sure that you can't get food poisoning from a handful of salted popcorn. Flushing the toilet, I splash cold water on my face and turn around to grab a towel when I spot Lianna standing in the doorway.

'Merry Christmas!' She whispers, her huge smile disappearing as she takes in my drawn appearance. 'You look terrible. Are you OK?'

'I'm fine.' I try to sound positive, but even speaking fills me with an over-powering nausea.

'Have you been sick?' Slipping into the bathroom, she closes the door silently behind her. 'You have, haven't you?'

'Just a bit, but I'm fine now.' I try to get

past her, but she puts her hand on the door handle. 'Honestly, Li. I'm fine.'

'I didn't notice you drinking much last night.'

'That's because I didn't. I only had a tiny glass.'

'Then why are you throwing up? You aren't ill, are you?' Lianna squints her eyes at me suspiciously and folds her arms. 'What is it? Salmonella? Malaria? Gout?'

'No! No! And no! Seriously, I am OK.' I attempt a laugh which comes out more of a cry. 'Let's go back to bed before we wake the entire apartment block up. It's not even light outside yet.'

Moving her out of the way, I put the towel into the laundry basket and open the door, but Lianna doesn't follow. 'Aren't you going back to bed?'

'You're not... *pregnant*, are you?' Her eyes sparkle as she speaks.

'No!' Panicking that someone might hear her, I quickly close the door and flip the lock. 'Do you mind keeping your voice down? Anyone could hear you!'

'Are you sure?' She presses, her voice still far too loud.

'Yes!' I yell, feeling sicker than ever.

'There's not even a *tiny* possibility? Because it just takes one time...'

'Lianna! I am fully aware of how babies

are made, thank you very much.' A little flustered at her outrageous accusation, I take a seat on the edge of the bath and try to calm down.

'Have you taken a test?'

'No!' I squeal.

'Why not?'

'Because I don't need to!' This is getting farcical.

'It wouldn't hurt to rule it out. When is your period due?' Li crosses her legs and puts on her serious face.

'Any day now and being sick a few times doesn't mean pregnancy. Talk about putting two and two together and coming up with a million.' I laugh nervously, but my mental menstrual calendar tells me that my monthly visit from Mother Nature should have arrived by now.

'Wait a minute. *A few times?* You have been sick more than once?' Lianna jumps to her feet and grabs my arm. 'That's it, you're taking a test.'

* * *

'This is absolutely insane.' I grumble under my breath.

If you would have told me yesterday that I would be walking to the newsagents at 7.30am on Christmas morning to get a pregnancy test, I never would have believed it. Weirdly, the snowy weather that we have become so accustomed to this December seems to have vanished and for the first time in a long time, I can actually see blue skies overhead.

Linking her arm through mine, Lianna waves the test in my face. 'What if it's positive?'

'It won't be.'

'It *might* be...'

I let out a tired sigh and shake my head in response. 'I just can't believe that Alan was even open today.'

'Alan doesn't celebrate Christmas. He converted to Buddhism last summer, remember?'

'Oh yeah...' I reply, although I don't have a clue what she is talking about. 'We should hurry up. I don't want Oliver to wake up and notice that we are missing.'

Increasing our pace to a light jog, we reach the apartment in no time and ride up to my floor in silence, both of us staring at the pregnancy test in my hand. Thankfully, the apartment is still in perfect silence, just as we left it. Safe in the knowledge that everyone is still in the land of nod, we slip into the bathroom and lock the door behind us. Ripping the packaging open, I tear the lid of the stick and try to think of crashing waves and heavy rainfall. The last time I took one these things it took me forever to generate a few drops of pee.

'Aren't you going to read the instructions?' Li asks, retrieving the wrapper from the bin.

'I'm pretty sure that there's only one way to do this.' Rolling my eyes, I take the plunge and pee on the stick.

Replacing the cap, I place it on the windowsill and proceed to wash my hands. Even though I know that the result will be negative, I still have a rather uneasy feeling in the pit of my stomach. Adrenaline? Fear, maybe? I fiddle with the band of my wedding ring as Lianna studies her watch closely. Come on! Shouldn't it be done by now? I pace back and forth in the bathroom for what seems like an eternity before snatching the test from the windowsill.

'Wait!' Lianna yells. 'It's not ready for another thirty seconds!'

Ignoring her cries, I turn over the stick and stare in the little window.

'It's negative.'

'It is?' She pops her head over my shoulder and takes a look for herself. 'Oh...'

As we stare at the stick intently, I blink in amazement as the single blue line multiplies before my eyes. 'What's happening? Is that... does that mean?'

'OMG! I *told* you that it wasn't ready yet!' Grabbing the instructions, Li compares the results to the paper and nods to confirm my suspicions. 'I knew it! I *knew* it.'

My stomach churns violently and I have an awful feeling that I am going to projectile vomit again. *I'm pregnant.* The words echo around my mind like thunder. *Pregnant! Me!* I look up at Lianna who is beaming down at me widely.

'I think I am going to be sick.' I announce, pushing her out of the way. 'I am. I'm going to be sick.'

'Clara?' Oliver's tired voice pierces my thought bubble and makes me freeze to the spot. 'Where are you?'

I lock eyes with Lianna who shoves the test into the bathroom cabinet and kicks it closed.

'I'm just using the bathroom!' I squawk, feeling panic start to take over my body. 'One minute!'

I run my hands through my hair and try to compose myself. 'What am I going to do?'

'Go.' Lianna laughs. 'Go and tell him!'

Nodding in response it takes me a few moments to regain the use of my feet,

which understandably appear to have
turned into stone. I really don't believe this
is happening. I feel like I have slipped into
a parallel universe. Sensing my fear,
Lianna reaches over and wraps her arms
around my neck.

'Everything will be OK, Clara. I promise.'

'Pinky-promise?'

I hold out my finger and she links it with
mine.

'Pinky-promise.'

* * *

I'm pregnant. I have reiterated those
two little words to myself all morning and
yet somehow it still doesn't seem any more
real. Aren't expectant mothers meant to be
glowing and beaming with joy? So far, the
only feelings that I have are fear,
trepidation and sheer terror. The very
moment that I climbed back into bed with
Oliver this morning I promised myself that
I would tell him, but for the life of me I just
couldn't bring myself to say it. Why? I have
no idea. Then I was going to tell him whilst
exchanging our presents, but the phone
rang and then the moment passed. *I am
pregnant.* I mean, how hard can it be?

Now I am chopping potatoes in the
kitchen and yet unbelievably I *still* haven't

told him. With all the excitement of Christmas Day, I haven't managed to get Lianna alone since I left her in the bathroom this morning. However, she has been staring at me gooey eyed all morning and I am starting to worry that she is going to let the cat out of the bag.

Listening to the chatter in the room, I look down at my stomach and try to imagine the little bean that is growing inside me. I still don't believe it. For around an hour this morning, I actually convinced myself that perhaps we had misread the test. I even sneaked off to the bathroom to look at the stick again, but there it was, the same double blue line that I saw this morning.

Isn't it strange how sometimes life throws something at you that puts everything else into perspective? After all my worrying about hosting the perfect Christmas Day, now it couldn't be further down my list of priorities. What does it matter what we eat, where we sit or what wine we serve? The only thing I can think of right now is that there is an actual baby in my belly. A baby that will eventually become a child. A child just like Madison or MJ. For what seems like the millionth time that day, I get the overwhelming urge to hurl.

Abandoning my potatoes, I leave the rest of the gang to do the cooking and slip out onto the balcony. Just like this morning, the sun is peeping through the clouds, melting the remnants of the snow on the ground. Breathing in the cold air, I fiddle with the sleeves of my reindeer jumper anxiously. I'm just going to have to spit it out, like ripping off a plaster, quick and painless. He is my bloody husband for crying out loud. It's not like he is a one night stand that I regret sorely.

'There you are.' As if reading my mind, Oliver appears behind me. 'Dinner is almost ready. Mom burned the parsnips, but apart from that, we are good to go. See, I *told* you that we could pull this off.'

I offer him a queasy smile and take a deep breath. *Tell him now! Tell him now!* The words scream in my mind's eye, so loud that I'm actually surprised that he can't hear them, too.

'Is everything OK?' He asks, slipping an arm around my waist. 'Is it the gift? Don't you like it?'

'No!' I glance down at my stunning new necklace and twist it around my fingers nervously. 'I love it.'

The only thing I don't like about the pretty platinum chain is that it makes my measly gift set look even more pathetic.

My heart pounds fast as I look up into Oliver's big blue peepers. I *have* to tell him. Out of the corner of my eye, I spot Lianna hovering around in the living room. She flashes me the thumbs up sign before disappearing out of sight.

I feel a rush of butterflies in my stomach as I gear myself to spit out what I have been trying to say all morning. When you think about it, what is more perfect to give your husband on this special day than the gift of life? Yes, it might be unexpected, but it most definitely not unwanted. Oliver is going to be a dad! I am going to be a mum! Without warning a dawning realisation sweeps over me. We are going to be... *parents!* Adrenaline soars through my body and I suddenly want to shout it from the rooftops.

'Follow me.' Taking him by the hand, I lead him through the apartment and into the bathroom.

'What's going on?' Looking rather puzzled, he allows me to drag him across the living room.

My entire body tingles as I lock the door and tell him to take a seat.

'OK...' He exhales slowly, an unreadable expression on his face. 'You're freaking me out now... what is it? If it's the necklace, just say and I'll return it first thing tomorrow. No biggie.'

'Oliver, for the last time, it is *not* the necklace.' My mouth goes inexplicably dry as I sit down next to him on the edge of the bath.

The sound of Wham! - Last Christmas drifts under the door and I know that if I don't tell him now then the moment will be lost once again.

'I'm pregnant.'

The words that escape my lips are barely above a whisper and judging by the expression on his face, I don't think that he has heard me.

'I'm... *pregnant*.' I repeat, a little louder.

He opens his mouth to speak, but no words come out. Not knowing what else to do, I run to the bathroom cabinet and grab the pregnancy test from earlier.

'We're going to have a baby.' I place the stick into his hands and hold my breath. 'Well, say something... please.'

'Pregnant?' A slow smile creeps onto his face as he looks up at me. 'As in *pregnant*... pregnant?'

I nod in response as a single tear slips down my cheek. His eyes glaze over as he pulls me over to him and wraps his arms around my shoulders. For a while neither of us say anything, we just hold each other closely, a strange excitement buzzing between us as we stare at the stick.

Planting a soft kiss on my nose, he holds me tightly against his chest. 'Clara... this... this is the best gift anyone has ever given to me.'

Untangling myself from his arms, I look deep into his eyes and get a glimpse of things to come. Ultrasound appointments, labour, sleepless nights, baby steps, those incredible first words. All of those things used to terrify me, but it's like someone has turned on a light. A light that says I was made for this, this is what I was put on this planet to do. Our wedding bands glisten under the bright bathroom lights and I suddenly have all the confidence I need to know that we are ready for this.

A light knocking on the bathroom door momentarily brings us out of our beautiful baby bubble.

'Dinner's on the table.' Lianna trills, rapping her knuckles on the door. 'Are you guys ready?'

I lock eyes with Oliver, my heart pounding as we answer simultaneously.

'We are...'

Christmas waves a magic wand over the world and suddenly everything is more beautiful...

To be continued...

Follow Lacey London on Twitter

@thelaceylondon

<u>Anxiety Girl is exclusive to Amazon.</u>

Meet Clara Andrews
Book 1

Meet Clara Andrews... Your new best friend!

With a love of cocktails and wine, a fantastic job in the fashion industry and the world's greatest best friends, Clara Andrews thought she had it all.

That is until a chance meeting introduces her to Oliver, a devastatingly handsome American designer. Trying to keep the focus on her work, Clara finds her heart stolen by Michelin starred restaurants and luxury hotels.

As things get flirty, Clara reminds herself that inter-office relationships are against the rules, so when a sudden recollection of a work's night out leads her to a cheeky, charming and downright gorgeous barman, she decides to see where it goes.

Clara soon finds out that dating two men isn't as easy as it seems...

Will she be able to play the field without getting played herself?

Join Clara as she finds herself landing in and out of trouble, re-affirming friendships, discovering truths and uncovering secrets.

Clara Meets the Parents Book 2

Almost a year has passed since Clara found love in the arms of delectable American Oliver Morgan and things are starting to heat up.

The nights of tequila shots and bodycon dresses are now a distant memory, but a content Clara couldn't be happier about it.

It's not just Clara things have changed for. Marc is settling into his new role as Baby Daddy and Lianna is lost in the arms of the hunky Dan once again.

When Oliver declares it time to meet the Texan in-laws, Clara is ecstatic and even more so when she discovers that the introduction will take place on the sandy beaches of Mexico!

Will Clara be able to win over Oliver's audacious
mother?

What secrets will unfold when she finds an ally
in the beautiful and captivating Erica?

Clara is going to need a little more than sun,
sand and margaritas to get through this one...

Meet Clara Morgan
Book 3

When Clara, Lianna and Gina all find themselves engaged at the same time, it soon becomes clear that things are going to get a little crazy.

With Lianna and Gina busy planning their own impending nuptials, it's not long before Oliver enlists the help of Janie, his feisty Texan mother, to help Clara plan the wedding of her dreams.

However, it's not long before Clara realizes that Janie's vision of the perfect wedding day is more than a little different to her own.

Will Clara be able to cope with her shameless mother-in-law Janie?

What will happen when a groom gets cold feet?

And how will Clara handle a blast from the past who makes a reappearance in the most unexpected way possible?

Join Clara and the gang as three very different brides, plan three very different weddings.

With each one looking for the perfect fairy tale ending, who will get their happily ever after...

Clara at Christmas
Book 4

With snowflakes falling and fairy lights twinkling brightly, it can only mean one thing - Christmas will be very soon upon us.

With just twenty-five days to go until the big day, Clara finds herself dealing with more than just the usual festive stresses.

Plans to host the perfect Christmas Day for her American in-laws are ambushed by her BFF's clichéd meltdown at turning thirty.

With a best friend on the verge of a mid-life crisis, putting Christmas dinner on the table isn't the only thing Clara has got to worry about this year.

Taking on the role of Best Friend/Therapist,

Head Chef and Party Planner is much harder than Clara had anticipated.

With the clock ticking, can Clara pull things together - or will Christmas Day turn out to be the December disaster that she is so desperate to avoid?

Join Clara and the gang in this festive instalment and discover what life changing gifts are waiting for them under the tree this year...

Meet Baby Morgan
Book 5

It's fair to say that pregnancy hasn't been the joyous journey that Clara had anticipated. Extreme morning sickness, swollen ankles and crude cravings have plagued her for months and now that she has gone over her due date, she is desperate to get this baby out of her.

With a lovely new home in the leafy, affluent village of Spring Oak, Clara and Oliver are ready to start this new chapter in their lives. The cot has been bought, the nursery has been decorated and a name has been chosen. All that is missing, is the baby himself.

As Lianna is enjoying new found success with her interior design firm, Periwinkle, Clara turns to the women of the village for company. The once inseparable duo find themselves at different points in their lives and for the first time in their friendship, the cracks start to show.

Will motherhood turn out to be everything that Clara ever dreamed of?

Which naughty neighbour has a sizzling secret that she so desperately wants to keep hidden?

Laugh, smile and cry with Clara as she embarks on her journey to motherhood. A journey that has some unexpected bumps along the way. Bumps that she never expected...

<u>Clara in the Caribbean</u>
<u>Book 6</u>

Almost a year has passed since Clara returned to the big smoke and she couldn't be happier to be back in her city.

With the perfect husband, her best friends for neighbours and a beautiful baby boy, Clara feels like every aspect of her life has finally fallen into place.

It's not just Clara who things are going well for. The Strokers have made the move back from the land down under and Lianna is on cloud nine – literally.

Not only has she been jetting across the globe with her interior design firm, Periwinkle, she has also met the man of her dreams... again.

For the past twelve months Li has been having a long distance relationship with Vernon Clarke, a handsome man she met a year earlier on the beautiful island of Barbados.

After spending just seven short days together, Lianna decided that Vernon was the man for her and they have been Skype smooching ever since.

Due to Li's disastrous dating history, it's fair to say that Clara is more than a little dubious about Vernon being 'The One.' So, when her neighbours invite Clara to their villa in the Caribbean, she can't resist the chance of checking out the mysterious Vernon for herself.

Has Lianna finally found true love?

Will Vernon turn out to a knight in shining armour or just another fool in tin foil?

Grab a rum punch and join Clara and the gang as they fly off to paradise in this sizzling summer read!

Clara in America
Book 7

With Clara struggling to find the perfect present for her baby boy's second birthday, she is pleasantly surprised when her crazy mother-in-law, Janie, sends them tickets to Orlando.

After a horrendous flight, a mix-up at the airport and a let-down with the weather, Clara begins to question her decision to fly out to America.

Despite the initial setbacks, the excitement of Orlando gets a hold of them and the Morgans start to enjoy the fabulous Sunshine State.

Too busy having fun in the Florida sun, Clara tries to ignore the nagging feeling that something isn't quite right.

Does Janie's impromptu act of kindness have a hidden agenda?

Just as things start to look up, Janie drops a bombshell that none of them saw coming.

Can Clara stop Janie from making a huge mistake, or has Oliver's audacious mother finally gone too far?

Join Clara as she gets swept up in a world of fast food, sunshine and roller-coasters.

With Janie refusing to play by the rules, it looks like the Morgans are in for a bumpy ride...

Clara in the Middle
Book 8

It's been six months since Clara's crazy mother-in-law took up residence in the Morgan's spare bedroom and things are starting to get strained.

Between bringing booty calls back to the apartment and teaching Noah curse words, Janie's outrageous behaviour has become worse than ever.

When she agreed to this temporary arrangement, Clara knew it was only a matter of time before there were fireworks. But with Oliver seemingly oblivious to Janie's shocking actions, Clara feels like she has nowhere to turn.

Thankfully for Clara, she has a fluffy new puppy

and a job at her friend's lavish florist to take her mind off the problems at home.

Throwing herself into her work, Clara finds herself feeling extremely grateful for her great circle of friends, but when one of them puts her in an incredibly awkward situation she starts to feel more alone than ever.

Will Janie's risky behaviour finally push a wedge between Clara and Oliver?

How will Clara handle things when Eve asks her for the biggest favour you could ever ask?

With Clara feeling like she is stuck in the middle of so many sticky situations, will she be able to keep everybody happy?

Join Clara and the gang as they tackle more family dramas, laugh until they cry and test their friendships to the absolute limit.

Clara's Last Christmas
Book 9

The series has taken us on a journey through the minefields of dating, wedding day nerves, motherhood, Barbados, America and beyond, but it is now time to say goodbye.

Suave. It's where it all began for Clara and the gang and in a strange twist of fate, it's also where it all ends...

Just a few months ago, life seemed pretty rosy indeed. With Lianna back in London for good, Clara had been enjoying every second with her best friend.

From blinged-up baby shopping with Eve to wedding planning with a delirious Dawn, Clara and her friends were happier than ever.

Unfortunately, their happiness is short lived, as just weeks before Christmas, Oliver and Marc discover that their jobs are in jeopardy.

With Clara helping Eve to prepare for not one, but two new arrivals, news that Suave is going into administration rocks her to the core.

It may be December, but the prospect of being jobless at Christmas means that not everyone is feeling festive. Do they give up on Suave and move on, or can the gang work as one to rescue the company that brought them all together?

Can Clara and her friends save Suave in time for Christmas?

Join the gang for one final ride in this LAST EVER instalment in the series!

Anxiety Girl

Sadie Valentine is just like you and I, or so she was...

Set in the glitzy and glamorous Cheshire village of Alderley Edge, Anxiety Girl is a story surrounding the struggles of a beautiful young lady who thought she had it all.

Once a normal-ish woman, mental illness wasn't something that Sadie really thought about, but when the three evils, anxiety, panic and depression creep into her life, Sadie wonders if she will ever see the light again.

With her best friend, Aldo, by her side, can Sadie crawl out of the impossibly dark hole and take back control of her life?

Once you have hit rock bottom, there's only one way to go...

Lacey London has spoken publicly about her own struggles with anxiety and hopes that Sadie will help other sufferers realise that there is light at the end of the tunnel.

The characters in this novel might be fictitious, but the feelings and emotions experienced are very real.

Made in the USA
San Bernardino, CA
13 November 2017